Restless Tides

Kelly Adams

Thorndike Press • Chivers Press
Waterville, Maine USA Bath, England

This Large Print edition is published by Thorndike Press, USA and by Chivers Press, England.

Published in the U.S. by arrangement with Maureen Moran Agency.

Published in the U.K. by arrangement with the author.

U.S. Softcover   0-7862-4417-8 (Paperback Series)
U.K. Hardcover   0-7540-7409-9 (Chivers Large Print)

The text of this Large Print edition is unabridged.
Other aspects of the book may vary from the original edition.

Set in 16 pt. Plantin by Al Chase.

Printed in the United States on permanent paper.

British Library Cataloguing-in-Publication Data available

ISBN 0-7862-4417-8 (lg. print : sc : alk. paper)

For Daryl —
with love

chapter

1

Cold, gray November light crept over the Chesapeake Bay and Tilghman Island as dawn broke, but there was no promise of warmth. Kate Flannery pulled her red knit cap down lower over her ears and slapped her gloved hands together briefly. She swung aboard her 35-foot skiff, the *Kathryn D*, and opened the door of the small cabin to toss in the new can of coffee and the bag of sandwiches and snack cakes.

"You're gettin' an early start this mornin', Katie," a voice called from the dock as she emerged from the cabin. She looked over to find one of the men from the skipjacks heading for his own boat. "You tongers lead a life of leisure," he added with a grin. "Everyone knows most of 'em sleep till pretty near nine. Not like us drudgers."

Kate returned the smile and nodded. "I hear the only reason you drudgers start so early, Mike, is because the taverns kick you out by daybreak."

Mike hooted in laughter as he hopped aboard his boat. "I swear, Katie, you're as sharp-tongued as your grandpa. How's that old dog doin', anyway?"

"He's ready to start a revolt in the rest home." She sighed ruefully. "Swears the doctor made a mistake, and his leg's not really broken."

Other oyster dredgers stepped out of the morning mist, joining in Mike's laughter. "I reckon he's probably right," Mike said. "I swear that old man is made of iron, not flesh and bone like the rest of us poor mortals."

"Katie's got to be made of some of the same stuff," a big ruddy-faced man called as he clambered into Mike's boat. "Only woman I know out tongin' oysters."

"Yeah, her grandpa raised a tough one," Mike agreed with another grin in her direction. "Probably fed her nails. Ain't that right, Kate?"

"Say, Katie," another man called, "my Peg and I thought that letter of yours in the newspaper was a right smart piece of writing."

"Yeah, fine job, Kate," another voice said. "About time someone spoke up for the watermen."

She smiled her thanks and went about priming her motor as the men bantered back and forth. It was like this every morning as the oyster dredgers, called drudgers by the locals, prepared to start the day.

Being out here on the bay in the misty sunrise was well worth the loss of sleep in a warm bed, she thought appreciatively as she looked down the dock at the line of old, weathered sailboats — called skipjacks — the dredgers used. Most sported new coats of paint and sails for the winter season ahead. Many were over seventy years old and had seen more of the bay than most men. It was like living in a piece of history, she thought dreamily, history written with tall masts and colorful bowsprits. A one-hundred-year-old Maryland law decreed that all oyster dredging had to be done with boats under the power of sail only. So these men, their fathers before them, and their grandfathers before them spent the winter months dredging oysters from skipjacks. It was a hard life, and few made much money from it, either dredging or tonging, but watermen were a breed apart. Like her grandfather said, the bay got into your blood.

Once the engine was ready, Kate got a butterscotch snack cake from the cabin and stood munching it on the deck, waiting for the mist to lift. She wiped icing from her mouth and glanced back into the cabin, wondering if she had enough time to make some coffee. Probably not, she decided regretfully. Catching her reflection in the glass of the cabin window, she automatically pushed an unruly piece of auburn hair under her cap. The chin-length blunt cut with full bangs made her look younger than her twenty-seven years, and she frowned, her blue eyes clouding. She should try to look more sophisticated. Then she dismissed the thought. What she looked like didn't matter to the bay. It wouldn't yield any more oysters even if she were wearing a black evening gown instead of the faded jeans, lined parka, and sturdy all-weather shoes. Unlike men, the Chesapeake didn't judge a woman on appearance.

"So there, Jeffrey," she muttered to herself. She shook her head in self-reproach. "You're definitely getting soft in the head, Kate," she said under her breath. "It's not bad enough that you talk to yourself. Now you're spouting off to your ex-husband, who's nowhere near here. Pretty soon you'll be babbling to the oysters."

"Hey, lady marine biologist!" The call came from the dock, and she swung her head to see her uncle standing there, hands on hips. "What are you doing — day-dreaming?" He laughed. "Won't catch oysters that way."

"Morning, Red," she called. "I expect you're right."

"Could you use an extra hand this morning?"

"You volunteering?" she teased him. "I thought you drudgers were spoiled by the easy life."

He grinned back at her and shook his head. "Not me. Tonging's too tough for me. But there's a young man here looking for some work."

Kate hadn't noticed the stranger who now stepped forward. Her eyes swept over him, and, as each detail of his appearance sank in, she felt a tickle grow in her stomach, as though her breakfast had turned to feathers. Rich brown curls escaped his black knit cap, falling casually over a broad, well-defined forehead. Hazel eyes fringed with thick, dark lashes stared back at her, but she could detect no emotion in them. She tried to force her attention back to Red, but instead she found her gaze drawn down the stranger's handsome, aristocratic face with its high cheekbones and square jaw, stopping a moment at the firm lips, then helplessly sliding over broad shoulders encased in a black windbreaker. Again she tried to tear her eyes away, but they insisted on following the line of the windbreaker down a long torso to tapered hips and finally to jeans that molded themselves to muscular thighs.

The jacket and jeans were definitely expensive. If this man was really a working waterman, then every unmarried woman on the Chesapeake would take up oyster tonging by morning. He looked like he belonged on a yacht, not an oyster skiff.

"Do I pass inspection?" he drawled coolly, making the question ring with sexual innuendo. Kate flushed, feeling like a co-ed caught gawking in the boys' locker room.

"I think I can get by without any help today," she said briskly, turning to glare at Red.

"I'll vouch for his character," Red said, winking over at the other men. "Besides, he needs the work."

She glanced back at the stranger and noted irritably that he was observing her openly, a mocking smile on his lips. "You aren't afraid of me, are you?" he asked.

Anger overrode her better judgment, and Kate snapped, "Afraid is hardly the correct word. Let's just say I'm skeptical of your ability to work."

She was dimly aware of Red covering a laugh with vigorous coughing. "You two'll get along fine," he chortled. "Kate Flannery, meet your new tonging partner, Jim. Now don't go pitching him overboard if he don't work hard enough to suit you."

His penetrating gaze swept her face as Jim swung aboard the skiff, and Kate felt the feathery tickling spread from her stomach up her spine. A purely physical reaction to an attractive man, she told herself. But the delectable sensation continued.

"You might make some coffee," she suggested in a business-like voice. "There's a propane stove in the cabin, and I just bought a new can. Some snack cakes there, too, if you want any."

She was relieved when he nodded and headed for the cabin. Kate cast off the rope, then idled the motor and started away from the dock, steering the rudder with a maneuvering stick at the stern. Around her, the skipjacks began to head toward the open water. Their sails down, they were nudged along by small motor-powered pushboats cinched to the stern. Once on the bay, the pushboats would be brought back on board and the sails raised.

The top half of the *Kathryn D*'s cabin was enclosed in glass, and from the rudder Kate could see Jim moving about inside making coffee. She judged him to be in his early thirties, though he had a look of experience about him, of competence. As though he'd felt her looking at him, he turned, and for a moment she was arrested by his hostile expression. He turned away again, and Kate stared at him in confusion. He'd been openly antagonistic since they'd set eyes on each other. Did he object to working for a woman? A lot of the watermen had the flu, and Jim could have easily found work on one of the skipjacks. It was almost as if he'd singled her out.

They were out on the bay now, and Kate hunched her shoulders against the chill wind. It promised to be a cold winter, but the beauty more than made up for any discomfort. The misty sunrise always exhilarated her, made her feel that she could take wing and fly across the water like an osprey looking for fish.

In the two years they were married, Jeffrey had never been able to understand her fascination with the bay and the life it offered. "Who would want to get up at the crack of dawn to ride in a cold boat, then spend hours doing back-breaking work, all for a few bushels of oysters?" he had grumbled the first time she'd taken him out on the *Kathryn D.*

Deep in her own thoughts, she was startled when she heard Jim's voice at her side. "Is that scowl for me? Or are you just naturally grumpy in the morning?"

"What is it with you?" she demanded, glaring at him. "Is someone forcing you to go oyster tonging with me?"

"Coffee?" he asked, ignoring her outburst, his eyebrows raised in mock politeness. Kate gritted her teeth as she took the mug.

Determined to match his cool exterior, she asked, "Is this your first tonging trip?"

He shook his head as his eyes scanned the water. "I did quite a bit as a teenager."

"Then you're not a waterman now?"

He shook his head again, leaving Kate to wonder what he did for a living.

"That man on the dock — Red — called you a marine biologist," he said unexpectedly.

She nodded. "I'm unemployed now," she murmured with a wry twist of her lips. "I was teaching in western Maryland, but I missed the Chesapeake area, so I came back last year and received a research grant to study the marine life in the bay. I had a lab at a wildlife facility at Easton."

"Had?"

Kate laughed without humor and stared

out at the horizon. "I was put out of business by economics. According to the Carlisle Foundation, the first commandment is, 'Ye shall put profit above all else.' My grant wasn't renewed this year. The money was poured back into petrochemicals."

Jim's mouth tightened, and one eyebrow rose as though something had just dawned on him. He exhaled slowly.

"Don't you keep anything for breakfast around here?" he demanded suddenly, and again Kate was caught off guard by his brusque manner.

"I take it you don't care for snack cakes."

"Not this early. I'm afraid my system isn't used to that kind of abuse."

"Then perhaps you'll be kind enough to tend the rudder," she retorted sweetly. "I'd like to go to the cabin and sink my teeth into some gooey, disgustingly unhealthy junk food." She intended to march away with supreme dignity, but as he reached for the rudder, his hand slid over hers, and she froze momentarily, blood rushing to her face. Despite the chill wind, warmth surged up her arm, and her stomach fell, as if she were on a roller coaster ride. She wrenched her hand away and stumbled to keep her footing as she hurried to the cabin.

His low laugh followed her. "Enjoy your breakfast," he called, but she detected a catch in his voice, as though the touch had cracked his cool demeanor.

She sat down at the cabin table and groaned. Propping her elbows on the table she rested her chin in her palms. Her stomach was still doing flip-flops, as though it was convinced that Jim was Mr. Wonderful, while her brain was screaming that he was overbearing and argumentative. When she saw Red again she was going to make it very clear just how she felt about his bringing Jim to her boat. Sure he was attractive, which was the logical explanation for her physical reaction to him, but barely a civil word had passed between them. Men!

She'd held them all at arm's length since the divorce — she didn't have time for them anyway. But she had the feeling that arm's length wouldn't be any distance at all to a man like Jim, if he set his mind on something. Well, there wasn't any need to worry about that — he would probably never want to see her again anyway.

When she emerged from the cabin he turned the rudder back to her without incident, and Kate guided the skiff into the Choptank River. Within minutes she had maneuvered them to an area over one of the public oyster bars. When the chunk of heavy metal that served as an anchor had disappeared into the water, she turned to Jim and said, "Gloves are in the oven, work apron on the chair." She peeled off her jacket, hoisted a pair of tongs from the work-deck, and turned, disconcerted to find Jim standing next to her.

"I'll tong," he said simply. "You can cull."

Kate tightened her grip on the tongs and shook her head. "I'll tong. You cull."

"Are you always this bossy, Miss Flannery?"

Kate flushed but refused to answer him, busying herself with pulling on her work gloves. Without looking at him, she moved to the side of the boat and lowered the long wooden handle of the tongs about seven feet to the oyster bar below. Then she moved back and forth, scooping oysters into the rake-like jaws.

Maybe it was Jim's presence or simply exhaustion, but the work seemed harder than usual. Oyster season had started at the beginning of November. Now there were only eight days until Thanksgiving, and Kate felt as if she had been tonging for a lifetime. Her shoulders and upper arms ached as she leaned over the boat, and she bit her lip to keep from groaning. Women's liberation or not, oyster tonging required the kind of muscles that the female physique got only from steroids. When she and her grandfather went out together she generally culled oysters while he tonged, but with his broken leg . . .

Kate began hauling aboard the first load of oysters, struggling to pull the heavy tongs from the water. She turned, half-expecting to find Jim standing idle, but he had set up the large work board that spanned the boat from side to side and was waiting in the oilskin apron and rubber gloves.

She dumped the oysters on the board and paused to rest a moment, watching him critically as he began culling them, her eyes intent on the table and his hands. Apparently he'd done this kind of work before. She took quick measurements of the oysters as he worked, noting with satisfaction that those in the pile of "keepers," those that would be marketed, were each longer than three inches from hinge to mouth. Jim used the chisel to break apart the oysters that were clumped together, then separated the small ones from the keepers.

Kate went back to work with the tongs, trying to find a comfortable rhythm. When she was alone she culled her own oysters, which gave her a rest from the backbreaking tonging. But with Jim culling efficiently, she had no reason to stop other than fatigue, and that was setting in quickly. She'd been working only a little over an hour, but her arms felt leaden, and her fingers were throbbing. The watermen called it "tongers disease," the painful stiffening of the hands that came after years of work on the cold bay. At this moment she felt as though she had an advanced case herself. Not only did her hands and arms hurt, but her back was also beginning to stiffen and ache from hauling aboard the heavy tongs with their harvest. She dumped the latest catch on the board and went back to the bow, slumping dispiritedly against the side to catch her breath. Perspiration had matted her hair to her forehead, and she was breathing heavily from the exertion.

"I'll take over for a while."

She looked up to find Jim standing next to her, holding out the gloves and apron. Her first impulse was to refuse his offer, and without thinking she said, "I'm fine." But under his wry surveillance she realized how pathetic and foolish her refusal sounded. "Thanks," she muttered in a low voice, taking the apron and handing him the tongs. Suited up in the apron and gloves, she sat at the work table and gratefully stretched her legs. Almost before she had caught her breath, Jim was dumping a load of oysters on the table, and she began culling. She worked almost automatically, her hands moving of their own accord, picking out the keepers with little conscious thought. Her eyes followed Jim's movements with grudging admiration. He stepped back and forth lithely in the even rhythm that became second nature to a waterman. He'd shrugged off his jacket, and she saw his shoulder muscles strain against his flannel shirt as he worked. Her mouth went suddenly dry, and she dropped her eyes back to the work table as he turned around with another load of oysters. The way her senses responded to him was irritating. How dare her subconscious find such an aggravating man attractive!

After a while, Kate glanced around and saw two other skiffs anchored over the oyster bar, their lone captains busy tonging. A look at the ascending sun suddenly made her realize that Jim had been tonging for almost two hours. When he dropped the next load on the board, she glanced up and said, "Want to break for some lunch?"

"More junk food?" he inquired wryly, his eyes mocking.

"This is civilization," she retorted in

brittle tones. "I always have a pitcher of martinis with my junk food at lunch."

Shooting him a dark look, she stood up and dropped the apron and gloves onto the deck. Jim's shirt and jeans were spattered with mud from the oysters, and she knew without looking that flecks of mud clung to her as well.

She emerged from the cabin a few minutes later with two cups of coffee and a brown bag. Jim was sitting on the deck, his back against the side of the boat, his forearms resting on his bent knees. He opened his eyes and brushed his arm across his forehead when she sat down a few feet away from him and handed him a cup of coffee. "I didn't know if you take cream or sugar," she said shortly.

He shook his head. "Black's fine."

She opened the bag and handed him one of the two sandwiches. Leaning back, she sipped her coffee and relaxed her cramped muscles, then took a bite of her sandwich and grimaced. The bread was stale. And after almost two weeks of the same menu, bologna sandwiches had begun to lose their charm.

"You really are a gourmet, aren't you?" Jim commented dryly. Kate darted him a malevolent look.

"If I'd known you were coming along, I'd have stayed up all night making fettucini."

"I'm sorry," he said, sighing heavily, and Kate stared at him openly. He'd actually apologized. "I know you packed this sandwich for yourself, and I appreciate your giving it to me."

"Well, the bread is stale," she admitted grudgingly. "I haven't had time to get to the store." Was he actually calling a truce?

"Don't you get any rest when you get through on the water?" he said. "You look worn out."

"I haven't had much sleep since oyster season opened," she admitted, taking another sip of coffee. "When I finish here I go back to my lab and work on my projects. And, of course, I have to check on my grandfather."

"Where's your lab? I thought the hateful Carlisle Foundation killed your grant."

"They did. But I moved my equipment to the house. I use a spare room off the kitchen."

"And your grandfather? Is he there?"

She shook her head and swallowed a mouthful of her sandwich before speaking. "He broke his leg in September, and the doctor ordered him to a rest home until it heals. The doctor knew if he let him go home, Buck would be out in a boat the first chance he got. Then he'd probably fall overboard, cast and all."

"Is that what you call him — Buck?"

Kate laughed. "He wouldn't answer to any other name. Actually, his given name is John, but when I was a little girl he gave me pony rides on his knee. I was always telling him to 'buck, buck.' He got a kick out of that, and gradually it became his nickname."

"It sounds like you have a close relationship with him."

Kate smiled. "He's the only family I've ever known. Buck raised me after my parents were killed in a car crash. I was just a baby then. My grandmother died not long after that, and everyone said a single, older man couldn't bring up a baby. But he did it. I never lacked for his time or his love."

"He sounds like quite a man."

"He is. He's threatening to take that nursing home apart unless they let him out." She laughed softly, then fell silent, drinking her coffee. "What about you?" she asked at last. "What made you come back to oystering?"

"This is just a vacation," he answered quietly. "I used to work on the bay years ago when I was in school, and I miss it."

"Where do you work now?"

"North of here," he said vaguely. "I have a dull office job."

He didn't volunteer any more information, and Kate sat quietly, watching him furtively. His set face was in profile, and his rough-hewn features were grim, giving the impression of a man preoccupied with his own thoughts. He stretched out his legs lazily, and Kate followed the movement. Again, she felt the stirring of an almost-forgotten longing and mentally chided herself. He would be gone after today or the day after that. Part-time watermen never stayed. She didn't know why she felt drawn to him, but she couldn't let herself dwell on it. Chalk it up to being without a man for too long.

"Well, we'd better get back to work," Kate sighed, standing up and moving toward the discarded tongs. Her leg brushed Jim's, and she tried to hide her momentary loss of equilibrium with a frown as she surveyed the pile of keepers. Brusquely she noted, "Another couple of hours and we should have twenty-five bushels."

"I'll do that," Jim said in a low voice, taking the tongs from her. "You cull."

"I want to do my share," she insisted stubbornly. "You've done most of the tonging."

"From the look of things you've done all the tonging for the past couple of weeks," he said. "And you're about to drop on your feet. You can use the break."

As she took her place at the work table, she had to admit it was a relief to give her shoulders and arms a rest. He was right — she was exhausted. But she needed money to pay for the rest home where Buck was recuperating, and oystering provided their only source of income. She had to make money while she could. If it was a hard winter the bay might freeze, and there might not be any oystering for a while. And that meant no money.

Kate had applied for three job openings in her field — all in teaching and not the research she loved — but there had been no replies yet, and she figured she'd better count on tonging until spring.

She glanced up as Jim dumped the first load onto the table. The sight of his shirt stretched over corded arm muscles sent her stomach on another roller coaster ride. She felt heat suffusing her face as he studied her. Then he swallowed and turned away.

An hour later Kate looked over the pile of oysters on deck and estimated that they had more than twenty-five bushels — a good day's work. She nodded to Jim, who set down the tongs and stretched, massaging his arms.

They hefted the anchor and started the engine. Kate turned the skiff around and headed back up the bay. Jim and Kate stood together in the stern watching the marsh grass and small inlets as the boat glided by them.

Kate was beginning to enjoy the serenity and the tenuous truce between her and Jim when a smokestack came into view on the distant shore. She gestured toward it in disgust. "Another carbon monster," she said. "That plant dumped raw sewage into the river last year, and it seeped into the bay. No telling how many fish and oysters were killed."

She glanced at Jim in time to see his jaw tighten and eyes narrow. "And no doubt you quite righteously fired off one of your heated letters to the editor," he commented tersely. "I hope you included a few facts this time."

Kate sputtered in surprise. "Righteous? For your information, the only letter to the editor I wrote concerned Carlisle Refineries, and I certainly had my facts straight."

"Your letter was nothing but flaming rhetoric," he snapped. "You attacked one of the area's biggest companies for no good reason."

"No good reason?" Her voice rose angrily. "You don't call a major oil spill a good reason?"

He snorted in disbelief. "It wasn't a major spill, but you managed to make it sound like the death knell of the bay."

"I'm concerned about the bay and its marine life," she said, furious.

"This isn't concern, Miss Flannery," he said dryly. "This is pure propaganda." He jerked his wallet from his hip pocket and flipped it open, extracting and unfolding a piece of newsprint. "May I quote?" he said sarcastically. " 'And in the final analysis, we have to choose for the future. The Carlisle policy of corporate progress at any cost is stupidity. We have to pay sooner or later. Right now it's the Chesapeake paying for monsters like Carlisle Refineries. In the not-so-distant future, it will be we, the watermen, and our children, paying for the mistakes of corporate sludge spewers. The price will be a dead bay.' Signed, K. Flannery, Tilghman Island."

Kate grimaced. "I'll admit I was a bit impassioned, but I didn't overstate the case."

Jim laughed humorlessly. "That was the most irresponsible piece of writing I've ever seen. You didn't even bother to get the full story about the oil spill, Miss Flannery."

"I'm not a journalist," Kate said angrily. They were drawing near the dock, and she maneuvered the boat toward it. "But I'm a damned good marine biologist, and I'm not going to stand by silently while some dollar-hungry refinery turns the bay into a sewer."

"I can't imagine you remaining silent about much of anything," he retorted. "You're an opinionated, stubborn idealist."

Kate was in the midst of an angry reply when she cut the engine as the skiff nosed the dock. "And you're an arrogant, snobbish know-it-all!" In the ensuing silence, her words carried clearly, and every man standing nearby turned to look. Ignoring the curious stares, Kate stood glaring at Jim while a machine scooped the oysters up and weighed them. Jim's eyes never left her face. If his expression was any indication, he was just as angry as she.

The buyer totaled up thirty bushels and handed Kate one hundred and eighty dollars. She thanked him and grimly counted out sixty dollars, which she shoved into Jim's hand. "I think that's fair for your work today," she said, challenging him to disagree.

"I'm sure you wouldn't treat me unfairly," he said with cold mockery, pocketing the money without looking at it. He stared at Kate a moment longer, a trace of confusion in his frown, as though his anger was tempered by some other emotion that he didn't know how to deal with. Then he turned away abruptly.

"I imagine you'll be glad to retreat to your office once your vacation's over," she said coolly. "Whatever you do, it can't be remotely connected with the bay."

"I wouldn't say that," he said in a low voice. "According to you, I'm engaged in poisoning it." He swung onto the dock and turned to glare at her, hands on hips. "I'm a petroleum engineer, Miss Flannery. My name's Jim Carlisle."

chapter

2

Kate stared open-mouthed as Jim Carlisle's tall figure disappeared down the wharf, his stride lithe and angry. Her mouth moved, but no sound came out. He was a Carlisle by employment and by birth. No wonder he'd been so antagonistic toward her.

"How'd your new first mate work out?" a voice drawled with a chuckle. Kate turned dazed eyes on Red. "Was he a good worker?"

"He's Jim Carlisle," she breathed softly.

Red slapped his thigh and laughed. "Told you I could vouch for him. How'd you two get along?"

Kate began to recover from her surprise, her temper flaring as she surveyed her uncle. "You knew who he was!" she sputtered. "You set it up."

"I'm sorry, Katie," he said, his chuckle anything but contrite. "I just couldn't help myself. Jim Carlisle came around looking for a Mr. K. Flannery, and I couldn't resist putting the two of you on. I'll wager he got a bit of a shock himself when he saw you."

"Mmmm," Kate muttered noncommittally.

"Did you get any tonging done, or did the two of you argue all morning?"

"We got our share of oysters," she said, nodding toward the wharf. "Despite the arguing." Then another thought struck her. "He took the sixty dollars I paid him!"

That seemed to delight Red even more. "Now that's what I call turnabout," he chortled. "Kate Flannery paid money to a Carlisle."

But Kate barely heard him. Her eyes were on the figure at the other end of the wharf unlocking a white Porsche. Her lips tightened as she watched him. Jim could have at least told her who he was and given her the opportunity to refuse him permission to board her boat. He'd deceived her. And then he'd deliberately baited her about her views on Carlisle Refineries. Well, no doubt that had been his way of getting even.

The Porsche roared away, and Kate turned back to Red. "At least he was a hard worker," she muttered.

"That one, yes," Red agreed. "He and his father used to tong up north years ago. Coupla good watermen they were."

"A waterman in the Carlisle family?" she murmured in disbelief.

Red nodded. "I think his dad was tossed out of the family. Least that's the story I heard."

"What happened to him?"

"Drowned one winter."

Kate shivered, and Red sighed. "The son, Jim, was in school, and his dad was out alone. Fell overboard in them heavy work boots and oilskin apron. Didn't have a chance in these cold waters."

"Many a good man lost that way," she whispered grimly.

"Yeah. Too many."

Kate shifted her weight slowly. "Well, I guess I'd better go on by and see how Buck's getting along. See you tomorrow, Red."

"So long, Katie. Tell that old crab I'll drop by this weekend."

She waved and headed for her own car, then stopped after she'd opened the door and stared up the road in the direction the Porsche had taken. She resolutely put Jim Carlisle out of her mind and got in the car. There was no use wondering about him. She'd never see him again anyway. They came from different worlds.

By the time Kate had left the nursing home, grabbed a sandwich, and stopped at the small general store, it was almost six. She urged her old car down the narrow, winding road, honking her horn as she passed Mary Peterson scraping leftovers into a dog dish under her yard light. Mary was a good neighbor even if her only hobby was gossip.

As Kate's car pulled into her own drive, a big Chesapeake Bay retriever bounded off the porch to meet her.

"Hello, boy," she murmured, stroking his chocolate-colored curly hair. "Did you miss me?"

Once inside, Kate switched on a light and collapsed into a chair. Fudge nuzzled her leg sympathetically, and Kate smiled. "Dinner-time, isn't it? I wish I could teach you to use the can opener. You're about as helpful as Jeffrey was around the house. But twice as smart." Giving him a rueful smile, she got a can of dog food from the cupboard and opened it. Fudge was at the bowl, wagging his tail even before she dumped the contents in front of him. Kate sighed. "At least you're not as picky as some men I know." She tried to summon some justifiable anger at the thought of Jim Carlisle, but indignation rapidly faded at the memory of his strong hand on hers. "Dammit, Kate, forget him," she muttered. "And stop talking to yourself!"

★ ★ ★

A couple of cars and a pickup truck were parked at the dock when Kate arrived the next morning. She waved to Red and another man, who were both waiting by their cars for their crews to show up.

"Looks like your new first mate is late for his second day at work," Red called, his eyes twinkling.

Kate shot him a rueful glance. "I'm afraid I'm back to working solo."

"You tongers are just too damn independent," Red said with a pretense at seriousness. "Rather be alone than share your boat with another soul." He pulled the toothpick from between his teeth and tossed it to the ground. "A bunch of hermits," he added, his eyes alight with amusement.

"Mmmm," Kate murmured as she swung aboard the *Kathryn D*, too weary to return his banter.

After a moment of silence, Red said, "You hung over this morning, Katie? I swear, I never seen you so quiet."

"Just tired, I guess," she said, trying to smile as she tossed the bag of food into the cabin.

"Maybe you need some help then," Red said, and she detected a teasing note in his voice. "Seems like your first mate is going to show up after all."

Kate swung around. Her eyes swept past Red's face-splitting grin and settled on the white Porsche pulling up to the dock. She chewed her lower lip, frowning, then turned back to the boat and began setting out the tongs. "You'd better hope your own crew shows up, Red," she called out, her voice suddenly light. "Though why they continue to work for a tyrant like you is beyond me."

Red's laughter split the still air. "Now there's the Katie I know. Seems like something perked you up. Ain't that right?"

Kate felt her cheeks grow hot, but she kept her face averted and tried to appear engrossed in her preparations. Perked up wasn't exactly correct. Girded for battle would describe her mood more accurately.

"Permission to come aboard, Captain?" It was Jim's voice, deep and quiet, with just a trace of mockery in it.

Kate straightened slowly and wiped her hands on her jeans. He was standing on the dock, a canvas bag hanging from his hand. Blue jeans molded his long, firm legs. Her eyes traveled up to the black windbreaker and then to his face, which had no hint of a smile. His brown hair framed his head in unruly curls.

She must be coming down with the flu, Kate thought vaguely. That could be the only explanation for the sudden tremor in her legs and the racing of her pulse. And that giddy smile you're suppressing with all your strength, she told herself. No breakfast, the reasonable side of her brain responded.

What was he doing here anyway?

"Are you planning to mutiny today?" she asked unsteadily. "I don't fancy being set adrift in a rowboat in the middle of the bay."

"No mutiny," he said quietly. "Although I'm sure if I tried, you'd be quite capable of clapping me in irons and tossing me in with the bilge pump."

Kate smiled wryly. "I think you overestimate me. Am I that intimidating?"

"You aren't the toughest captain I've heard of," he said. "They say Captain Hook was a terror — if you can believe the bad press Peter Pan gave him." His tone was deliberately mocking, and Kate grimaced, knowing he was referring to her attack on the refinery.

She shook her head. "I must be crazy, but come on aboard."

He stepped onto the skiff, and Kate pointed to the canvas sack. "What did you bring?"

"Oil cans."

"What?"

"Cans of oil from the refinery. When it comes to pollution, I like to bypass the middle man. I thought I'd just dump them in the bay myself, then you can write an eyewitness account."

She gave him a black look and went back to work on the tongs as he disappeared into the cabin. She could tell she wasn't going to get a straight answer from him. Why had he come back? Certainly not because they got along well.

The contents of the bag became apparent twenty minutes later as the *Kathryn D* edged out into the bay with Kate manning the rudder. Jim emerged from the cabin carrying a plate of food. He handed it to her as he took over the rudder.

"Scrambled eggs and sausage," she said in surprise, sitting down on the raised platform in front of the rudder stick. "You didn't tell me you could cook. I would have escorted you on board with more pomp and circumstance."

"I can whip up a few of the basics," he said, his eyes on the water. "And I was motivated."

"No doubt by the prospect of more cupcakes for breakfast?" she asked dryly.

"Something like that," he said, his eyes sweeping over her briefly.

Her skin tingled as if he had physically touched her, and she turned her gaze away from him. "Too bad," she said lightly. "You've never lived until you've tried my chocolate omelet."

"I'll bet," he said sarcastically. "But I've lived thirty-three years without heartburn, and I think I can wait a while longer."

So he was thirty-three. Kate studied his face through her lashes while his attention was on the bay. He certainly seemed at ease on the water, but then Red had said he used to tong with his father. It must have been hard on him, losing his father to the bay like that. But he looked like the kind of man who was strengthened by adversity. The firm set of his mouth and jaw didn't belong to someone who'd been defeated by trouble.

"Didn't you ever learn to cook?" he asked.

"I can cook," she asserted, "but right now I just don't have time. Now, if you really want to talk gourmet, you should try the croquettes Buck and I mix up. They're made from leftover anything. *Très élégante.*"

"You and your grandfather must be the culinary terrors of the eastern seaboard," he observed dryly.

"We try," she said, scraping the last of the sausage from her plate. "That was truly delicious."

39

"High praise from such a gourmet."

She studied the plate with its worn flower design and tapped it experimentally with her finger. Plastic. She caught his eye.

"The Carlisle family heirloom china," he offered.

"Right. Now, why don't you go eat some breakfast yourself? I'll take over the rudder."

He nodded and disappeared into the cabin with her plate. Kate allowed herself a smile. A man who could cook his own breakfast had at least one redeeming talent. And he wasn't without a certain grim sense of humor.

But he was still a Carlisle.

Sometime later they anchored at the mouth of the Little Choptank River. Mellowed by the breakfast and the beautiful morning, Kate looked around appreciatively. Sky and bay melded in the faint pinks and purples of early sunrise, and the dusky shoreline remained shrouded in mist. The call of a whistling swan carried across the water, announcing the end of night, and Kate felt a shiver of pleasure in the exquisite loveliness of it all. She glanced at Jim and read the same admiration in his eyes. "Out on the water it's like the beginning of the world every day," he said softly.

She was bemused by his comment and began setting out the tongs, wondering what other dimensions there were to him.

Jim insisted on doing the tonging while Kate culled. As the sun rose higher in the sky, the pile of oysters on deck grew larger. Jim stopped now and then to wipe perspiration from his forehead, and Kate dabbed occasionally at the flecks of mud that spattered her face and hands.

It seemed only a short while later when she glanced up to find Jim standing in front of the work board, stretching. "A pretty good morning's work," he observed with satisfaction, regarding the pile of oysters. Kate followed his gaze and noted with surprise that it was indeed a good catch. She looked at her watch and stood up, brushing off her hands.

"I didn't realize it was so late. You must be starved." She moved the work board and stretched her own cramped muscles.

He was massaging his upper arms, and Kate's throat constricted as she watched the lean, long fingers. Her brain, no doubt feverish with the flu, was creating vivid sensations of coiled heat in her stomach as she imagined how those fingers would feel on her shoulders, her back, her legs . . .

"Watch out!"

His warning jerked Kate from her reverie,

but not in time to keep her from tripping over the spare set of tongs on the deck. She felt her feet fly out from under her, but before she could fall he was beside her, his hand gripping her arm. It seemed only natural that his other hand moved to her back as he steadied her. She found herself standing only inches away from him, so close that she could feel the warmth from his body. Neither of them moved, and when she dared look up at him, she felt his hands tighten on her. His expression softened, and Kate's breath caught as his fingers lightly stroked the hair at the nape of her neck. Delicious shivers raced through her, and November seemed to turn suddenly into July.

He removed his hands slowly, watching her a moment longer with an intense expression. "I'll get lunch," he said hoarsely, and Kate let out a deep breath as he disappeared into the cabin.

Either they were both coming down with the flu or . . .

She didn't want to dwell on the "or else" because it complicated her life at a time when she couldn't afford another complication. But her pulse was still rapid when she headed for the cabin.

She washed her hands in the tiny cabin sink and splashed water on her face as Jim began unloading the canvas bag. Cold fried chicken, potato chips, coleslaw, rolls, and two slices of cherry pie appeared on the counter in short order. Kate glanced covertly at the food as she hesitantly picked up her own lunch bag with its meager contents. He hadn't actually asked her to join him, but there *were* two pieces of pie. Still, she wasn't about to ask him if he would share.

"Your valet must have spent all night fixing that," she said finally, hoping she sounded off-hand.

He turned with two plates in his hand, a new gentleness on his face. "I'm afraid he was too busy pressing my numerous tuxedos," he parried. "Life around the mansion can be hectic." He handed her a plate. "Here, help yourself."

"Thank you," she said, her restraint disappearing. She was starving for the best food she'd seen or smelled since the winter oyster season had begun. She heaped her plate, then looked at him guiltily.

"I brought plenty," he reassured her. "I don't know how you have the stamina to do this kind of work on what you usually eat."

"I'm afraid that lately I haven't had the stamina to do much of anything, cooking included," she admitted. "You can't imagine how good this looks."

They sat down on wooden benches on opposite sides of the table. For several minutes Kate was too busy eating to talk. When she came up for air, she found Jim surveying the cabin.

"This is cozy. Do you spend the night on the skiff very often?"

She glanced at the small bed built into the side and shook her head. "Occasionally, if the oystering is especially good, Buck stays out all night. Or if a squall comes up, he docks at the nearest safe spot. It gets cold in winter, even in the cabin."

"I know," Jim said softly, and she remembered his father.

They ate in silence until Kate leaned back with a contented smile. "Thank you for the lunch. Now that I've been wined and dined and lulled into a false sense of security, tell me why you came back to the *Kathryn D*."

"The *Kathryn D*," he repeated quietly. "Is that your name?"

She nodded. "Kathryn Diane."

"So you have a boat named after you. Most impressive."

"Actually it's the other way around. I was named after the boat. Well, really after my mother and grandmother. My grandfather named his first boat the *Kathryn D* after my grandmother. The name was passed down

44

to my mother, then to me, and we've always had a boat with that name. Tradition."

"Tradition's nice."

"And you're evading my question," she prompted.

"Yes, well," he said with false enthusiasm, "I wanted to be sure you got at least one decent meal this winter." Then he shrugged and added more seriously, "I don't know. I suppose I felt I hadn't really given you a chance. I'd come to Tilghman Island looking for some crusty old waterman who'd maligned Carlisle Refineries, and instead I found a pretty young woman with a strong sense of justice. I felt I hadn't made a very good first impression."

"So you came back in the interest of public relations," she said. "Are you going to convince me that Carlisle Refineries is an industrial saint?"

"That might be asking the impossible of you," he admitted with a wry twist of his lips. He took a sip of coffee, then ran his hand through his hair in a weary gesture. "I don't know. I've been at loose ends lately, and I didn't relish the prospect of spending my vacation in my apartment. I thought working on the bay might be the answer. A return to my roots, or something like that."

"You sound like a victim of the divorce

court," she said with an attempt at humor. "Nothing gives you that lonely feeling like the final decree."

He shook his head. "No, not a divorce." He fell silent, and she saw that he was lost in his own thoughts. When he looked up again, the cloudiness was gone from the hazel eyes. "We'd better knock off this soul-searching and get back to the oysters."

They carried their plates to the counter. As Jim reached across Kate for the canvas bag, his hand brushed hers, and she felt another shiver of pleasure, as if he'd stroked her hair again. For an instant she thought his hand shook slightly, but it must have been her imagination.

Her pulse was still racing when they started back to work. She couldn't keep her eyes off Jim's body moving at the bow of the skiff, the corded muscles of his arms standing out against his flannel shirt as he hauled the oysters aboard.

They worked in silence for the rest of the afternoon, but it seemed to Kate that Jim lingered near the work board more and more.

When she finally turned the skiff toward home, Jim stayed at the bow, staring out at the passing shoreline.

At the wharf, Kate collected the money,

then automatically pushed seventy dollars toward Jim. When he didn't take it, their eyes locked. His were amused. "You earned it," she said stubbornly. "You did the hardest work."

"I'm not doing it for the money."

"That's not important," she insisted. "You deserve it. Please take it as a favor to me."

"All right," he said with a gentle smile, pocketing the bills. "Thank you. And now I'd like to ask a favor in return."

"Okay."

"I'd like to see your lab."

Kate drew in a deep breath and let it out slowly. His simple request stirred a tempest of emotions in her. She took pride in her work and enjoyed sharing it with others. But now her lab was in her home, and she wasn't sure she was ready to share that with anyone, least of all Jim. Just the thought of being alone with him there was enough to send her temperature sky-high again.

"I don't know," she began hesitantly.

"I promise not to spill any oil in your work. I'd really like to see it."

The calm, rational side of Kate's mind analyzed the situation dispassionately. This was simply a case of a man showing a little courteous interest in a woman's career. But the other part of her mind, the emotional side, was repeating, *You're out of his league.*

"Science triumphs," she murmured, then caught his puzzled frown and laughed. "I'm afraid I have a bad habit of talking to myself." She paused. "Well, do you want to follow me home?"

"Provided we make one stop first. I have a feeling you don't have a good dinner waiting for you at home."

Kate shook her head. "Right on target. Unless you've developed a taste for stale bologna sandwiches."

His groan confirmed that he hadn't.

They pulled into her driveway after a short stop at the general store, the white Porsche following Kate's vintage Ford. A joyful Fudge leaped from the porch as Kate approached, then moved tentatively to Jim and sniffed his leg. "Are you a friend of Miss Flannery's?" Jim asked in a soothing voice. When the dog wagged his tail, Jim rubbed his head with his free hand, his right holding the bag of groceries. That was all the encouragement the retriever needed. The next instant he was pawing Jim gleefully.

"That's Fudge." Kate laughed. "Come on in before his welcome gets any more enthusiastic. And please call me Kate," she added.

"Fudge?" Jim inquired once he'd set the groceries on the table. "You really do have a fixation on junk food, don't you?"

"I know your opinions of my dietary habits, Mr. Carlisle," she said with mock severity as she unpacked the groceries, "and tonight I'm going to prove you wrong."

"Hear that, fella?" Jim said, patting the dog. "You have to share your chow with me tonight."

Fudge gave him a quizzical look, as though trying to fathom what he'd said, and Kate laughed again. "Before I dazzle you with my kitchen wizardry, you get a tour of the lab."

She put the last of the food in the refrigerator, and Jim followed her through the hall into the lab. "This is it," she announced, turning on the light, "although I'm sure it pales by comparison with the facilities at the refinery." There was an edge to her voice as she remembered her disappointment when the grant had been canceled.

But Jim was stepping forward to inspect with apparent interest the rows of aquariums with their charts, beakers, and measuring instruments. "I've been working on salinity research," Kate explained, moving to stand beside him. "These are oyster spat here — young oysters. Tides and the rivers cause a wide variance in the bay's salinity. I'm working on the effect of different salinity levels on oyster growth."

"They're very resilient creatures, aren't they?" Jim commented, bending to look into the glass tanks.

Kate nodded. "They can withstand a lot of change and still thrive. If we can find optimum conditions for them, we can increase the harvest and even grow them outside the bay environment."

They moved on to other tables. Kate pointed out the chemicals she was testing on the spat and the effect temperatures had on growth.

When she looked up at Jim, she saw that he was smiling at her. "Am I rambling?" she asked apologetically.

"No," he said quickly. "This is fascinating. It's just that your face lights up when you talk about your work."

"I love it," she said immediately. "It's amazing to discover how tenacious life is and how precious." She dusted her hands briskly. "There. Enough of my talk. You can wash up in there if you want, and I'll start dinner."

When Jim returned to the kitchen, she was dredging pork chops in flour, then dropping them into the hot skillet. The savory aroma began to fill the room, and he sniffed appreciatively. "This feels like a real home," he said, putting his hands in his pockets and glancing around the room.

Kate smiled. It wasn't much, but she knew what he meant. Red gingham curtains at the windows and the braided rug on the red tile floor gave the room a warm look. The old oak kitchen table had been in her family for generations, and its scratched surface bore testimony to the years of life played out there. Kate felt her breath catch as she watched Jim run his hand over the worn tabletop. The gesture was intimate, and it suddenly struck her that he was the first man other than her grandfather and his friends who'd been in this house during the past year.

He walked toward her as she leaned against the stove. When he stopped in front of her the silence was broken only by the ticking of the mantel clock and the pork chops sizzling in the skillet. His eyes moved restlessly over her face and settled on her lips. Kate felt immobilized, her heart beating a staccato rhythm that pounded in her throat. She stared back at him, a wave of desire coursing through her blood like a powerful drug. She wanted to feel his hands on her again. She wanted to taste his lips, touch his hair, feel their bodies pressed together.

Don't think about what you want, she told herself. She'd carefully and deliberately put her own wants and needs on a back shelf for a long time now. She was afraid she'd want and need things she couldn't have if she let them come forward. Instinct told her that one touch from Jim would only fuel her desires, and when she was hopelessly hooked on him, he was liable to walk out of her life as quickly as he'd come into it.

Just one touch, argued her fevered heart as he moved closer to her. She closed her eyes heavily, giving in even as she cursed her weakness. His hands caressed her shoulders first, tracing gentle circles that made her tremble. Slowly they traveled to her throat, stroking it with infinite care, as if she might flee like a wild animal if he startled her. Her breath was coming in soft pants when she felt his lips touch hers, and with a muffled gasp she lifted her arms to his neck.

Her intuition had been right — the kiss aroused in her a longing as inescapable as quicksand. She'd fallen into a deadly, velvet trap. But at the moment, she didn't care. His lips demanded more and more of her, and she gave him what he wanted. She'd never felt such an intense reaction to a man before — he was a flame and she the kindling — and it frightened her even as he pulled her deeper under his spell, his tongue probing the moist recesses of her mouth.

A push at her leg rocked her away from Jim, and Kate opened her eyes in surprise. Fudge was standing beside her, wagging his tail and jumping playfully.

"Just what I need, a chaperone," Jim commented wryly, but a quick glance at him convinced Kate that he was joking. In fact, he seemed not at all disturbed by Fudge's interruption, or by the kiss for that matter.

"The pork chops," she mumbled, seizing on an excuse to ignore what had just happened. She turned back to the stove.

"How can I help?" Jim asked. "Tell me where the plates are."

Was he so adept at seduction that the kiss had meant nothing to him? The thought was appalling, and she quickly dismissed it. She forced a bright smile on her face and made her voice light as she opened the cupboard. "The Flannery family china," she said, taking out the chipped plates with their faded blue boat pattern.

"To go with the crystal," Jim added as he set out glasses that had once held grape jelly. "Now where do you keep the monogrammed napkins?"

"I'll get them." She located paper napkins in another cupboard, then on impulse pulled a pen from the drawer and drew a small F in the corner of each one. *"Voilà,"* she said, setting them on the table with a flourish.

"Now that's chic," he allowed. "Candles?"

After some searching, she produced two bright red candles left over from last year's Christmas. Jim lit them.

Kate dished up pork chops and green beans from the stove, then pulled biscuits from the oven while Jim poured the wine.

He held her chair for her, and silently they sat down to dinner by candlelight, Fudge curled up at their feet, keeping an eye out for leftovers.

Kate was putting on a mask of sophistication she didn't feel. They had just shared a kiss so explosive that her pulse was still thudding in her ears. They were eating dinner together in her kitchen, which at the moment felt even more intimate than a back booth in the best restaurant on the Chesapeake. And Jim Carlisle, who no doubt was more accustomed to pheasant under glass and champagne, was eating pork chops as if he was really enjoying them.

"To oyster tongers," he said, clinking his

wineglass against hers.

"And the Chesapeake."

"The Chesapeake," he agreed. "Kate Flannery's true love."

Kate coughed as her wine went down the wrong way. When her eyes stopped watering, she saw that Jim was regarding her gently.

"Weren't there ever any men in your life?" he asked. "Other than family."

Kate set her glass down carefully, because her trembling hand threatened to tip it over. Jim certainly believed in directness. "There was one," she said softly. "Jeffrey."

"And what happened to him?"

"He came into my life, and then he went back out of it again," she said quietly. "He was in love with another woman, but she married someone else, so Jeffrey married me. Then, when his real love shed her husband, Jeffrey left me to marry her. End of story."

"I'm sorry. That must have been difficult for you."

Kate shrugged. "It's only a memory now." It was true. From the first moment Jim's lips had claimed hers, Jeffrey's kisses had dwindled to nothing. He'd never touched her deeply the way Jim already had.

She looked across the table, disconcerted to

find him watching her carefully, as though he were seeing things she'd never shared with anyone.

"But you're not lonely, are you?" he asked.

"No, I'm not." She was glad he understood the distinction between lonely and alone.

Jim didn't question her further, and they ate the rest of the meal in silence. "I guess I ought to clean up these dishes," she said when he scraped back his chair and began clearing the table.

"No, you won't," he insisted. "I'm going to take care of these. You look exhausted. Go sit down in the other room and take it easy."

"Why don't you just leave them?" she suggested. "I can do them tomorrow."

"We'll compromise. Go sit down, and I'll just rinse them off."

"All right," she agreed. He escorted her to the living room and made sure she was sitting on the couch in front of the fireplace, then he returned to the kitchen.

Kate heard the dishes clink and smiled as she leaned her head against the couch. It was pleasant to just relax for a change.

He was right about her being exhausted, she thought, rubbing her forehead. The combination of her fatigue and the wine was making her eyelids heavy. She closed her eyes briefly and curled down deeper on the couch. Be careful, Kate, she told herself, Jim Carlisle's capable of turning your life upside down.

She must have fallen asleep, because she was dreaming she was being gently lifted into strong arms, her head cradled against a firm chest. Her hand fluttered up and touched a soft flannel shirt, and she murmured in contentment. She was too drowsy to protest when she was lowered onto something soft, and the strong arms left her. She reached out, and hands closed over both of hers, placing them back by her side. Lips brushed her cheek, and she smiled, letting herself drift deeper into her sweet dream.

chapter

3

Kate groaned when the alarm went off. She'd been dreaming that she was lying on a pile of oyster shells, and now her upper thigh ached. She threw back the covers and struggled to her feet, staring down at herself in surprise when she discovered that she was still wearing her jeans and shirt. No wonder she was sore! The car keys in her pocket had dug into her hip all night.

So it hadn't been a dream after all. Jim had carried her to bed. And the way she'd reached out to him — had that been a dream?

Abruptly a wave of irritation washed over her. Now he'd think she was the kind of weak-kneed female who enjoyed being tucked into bed like a child! She headed for the bathroom, her annoyance growing by the moment. She must have been exhausted to the point of lunacy last night to have fallen under his spell so thoroughly. She'd never lost control with a man before, and it wasn't going to happen again.

Kate ate a spoonful of peanut butter from the jar in the refrigerator, then pulled on her jacket. With one arm in the sleeve, she halted suddenly and stared at the sink. Jim had done the dishes and wiped the counter. Her annoyance flared anew. She headed for the door, grabbing a loaf of bread to take with her.

Kate shivered as she drove toward the dock, wishing her car would warm up faster. She'd planned to buy a new one this year if the Carlisle Foundation had renewed her research grant. Now all of her savings would have to support her research, and the best she could do for her old car was to get it a new battery, maybe for Christmas.

She felt another glimmer of irritation when she saw the white Porsche parked at the dock. She pulled up next to it, unrepentant when her door bumped the Porsche as she got out. As she leaned back onto the Ford to retrieve the bread she'd brought, her door grazed his car again, but she took little notice.

She was hurrying to her skiff, nodding and exchanging greetings with the dredgers, when Jim uncoiled his length from the dock piling where he'd been sitting next to her skiff. "Do you always play bumper cars in the parking lot?" he asked sardonically.

"Have your valet send me a bill for the damages," she replied crisply, catching the quick arch of his eyebrow as she brushed past him. He followed her on board without comment and stood watching as she put the bread in the small gas-powered refrigerator in the cabin. She avoided looking directly at him as she hurried to the deck to set out the tongs, but she noticed from the corner of her eye that he was unloading food from his own canvas bag into the refrigerator. She tightened her lips but said nothing.

Red waved at her cheerily from his skip-jack, which was moored next to her boat, and Kate returned the wave half-heartedly. "That new hand of yours a half-decent cook?" he called out in his rough voice. From another man the words would have been intimidating, but with Red everything seemed to come out sounding good-natured.

"He fancies himself one," Kate answered through gritted teeth, unable to shake the annoyance that had descended on her when she'd awakened that morning.

Red laughed. "You'd best watch your step then, Katie, my dear. As memory serves, you were the little girl who used to give out kisses for a piece of penny candy."

The men working around him on the skip-jack joined his teasing laughter, and for once Kate was left without a retort, feeling heat creep into her face.

As a little girl, she'd been the darling of the oyster dredgers when Buck would bring her to the dock. They'd teased, praised, and bribed her with penny candy — which was almost a nickel then — for a kiss, roaring in delight when she planted her mouth on each beard-roughened face. They were all uncles to her, by blood or by friendship, and they'd helped Buck raise her to be strong and independent.

She managed a tight smile, but it was Jim who answered Red's gibe. "Maybe you can recommend a candy store," he called back. "Nothing else seems to work."

Their laughter increased, and Kate managed to start the engine and maneuver the skiff toward the bay. As she turned the rudder, Red's voice floated across the water, ringing with amusement. "Maybe I ought to come along today to chaperone."

"All we're going to do is work, and that wouldn't suit an old drudger like you," Kate called back over her shoulder, her eyes fixed resolutely ahead as the boat nudged toward open water. Another burst of laughter followed her retort, which faded slowly as the skiff plowed away from the dock.

Red, Mike, and the other watermen had never liked Jeffrey, she remembered suddenly as she headed the *Kathryn D* toward the Choptank River. They had never come out and said so, but she'd sensed their disapproval. They'd addressed Jeffrey with cool politeness, never teasing him the way they did Jim. Even after their marriage, Jeffrey had remained an outsider. Now, looking back, she could understand why. He had shown nothing but disdain for the watermen and their ways, and he had never understood why Kate loved the bay. He had finally convinced her that she was clinging to her childhood and that she would be just as happy elsewhere. They had left the Chesapeake, and Kate had been miserable.

She broke off her reverie when Jim appeared beside her with a cup of coffee. He took the rudder, and Kate stretched her cramped shoulder muscles. She took a first sip, then stood transfixed as his hand touched the back of her neck, gently massaging. Suddenly she felt as though the boat had pitched beneath her, and she swayed slightly. But her own internal compass had malfunctioned, not the boat. Even after she'd had a good night's sleep, Jim had an overwhelming effect on her.

Afraid she would lose control, she stepped out of his reach and inhaled deeply. Those fingers had been so tantalizing . . .

"Your breakfast is on the counter." His voice was low and husky, and it made her ache for his touch again.

"I'm really not hungry."

"You'll be working hard today," he said, a sharp edge to his voice. "Go eat."

His peremptory tone rekindled her annoyance, and she tilted her chin defiantly. Reason argued that he was only being considerate, both last night and today, but her impulse was to rebel. Instead of arguing, she went to the cabin without another word. She was acting like a cranky child, meeting every kindness he offered with a snarl. What was wrong with her?

He anchored them over an oyster bar in the Choptank River while Kate set up the work table. Jim tonged. Only the clatter of oyster shells hitting the board punctuated the silence.

Kate offered to take over the tonging as the morning wore on, but Jim declined politely, and she went back to culling, her teeth clenched tight in anger.

He called a break for lunch when the sun was directly overhead. They washed up at the cabin sink.

"I hope you don't mind chicken again," he said, setting two plates on the table. "That's all the deli had last night."

"The deli?" she asked coolly as she took the seat opposite him. "Did your chauffeur pick up a carry-out bucket for you?"

Jim leaned back in his chair and eyed her speculatively. "No, my chauffeur did not. Nor did my valet."

Undeterred by the warning note in his voice, Kate continued snipping, detesting the shrillness of her voice, yet compelled to go on. "Then maybe the maid," she said. "Surely someone else must do all your work."

"Are you always so contrary, Kate?" he demanded in an icy calm voice. "We seemed to have a fairly good time together last night, and now all morning you've been acting as if I've committed some unforgivable sin. Would you mind explaining what's wrong?"

"Nothing's wrong," she snapped, her annoyance flaring again.

He shrugged. "If you don't want to discuss it, then I suggest you eat your chicken." He leaned forward as if the discussion were closed and began eating calmly.

"Will you stop telling me what to do!" Kate exploded angrily. "I don't want you feeding me every meal and telling me to eat!

64

I can do my own dishes, and I can do my own share of tonging." She stopped, out of breath. "And another thing — I don't want to be tucked in at night like a child!"

She glared at him across the small table, and to her surprise he began to smile, a slow smile that reached his eyes. "And what's so funny?" she demanded.

"I'm not laughing at you," he assured her quickly. "I got too close, didn't I?"

"What are you talking about?"

"You refuse to let anyone get within an inch of you, Kate. The minute someone does one little thing for you, you feel as if your independence is being threatened, and you back off like a frightened kitten. You won't let yourself trust anyone."

"That's not true," she retorted quickly. "I just don't like people interfering in my life."

"It's the same thing," he parried. "You hold everyone at arm's length so you can protect your image of yourself — the tough, competent female oyster tonger who can match the work of any man. That's what you think of yourself, isn't it, Kate?"

"No," she protested. "You wouldn't understand. You've lived a different life. You don't know what it's like to have a bad winter and wonder if you'll make enough money to pay the mortgage, to work part-time to help pay the bills. Then there was college. It isn't easy for oyster tongers to put their kids through school. But with Buck's help and my part-time job and a scholarship, I made it. Don't tell me what my self-image is, Jim Carlisle, because you don't know anything about it. You don't know about having to work on the bay, working because it's the only life you know or love, or about the men who get sick and can't work or who don't come back from . . ." She stopped suddenly, seeing pain flick in his eyes. She felt the blood drain from her face. *Why had she said that?* "I'm sorry," she said hoarsely.

Jim didn't say anything. He hid his pain behind a mask of cool boredom, but Kate had seen the effort it took to hide it, and she knew it was a thin disguise.

She stood up and started for the door. "I'm not very hungry," she said quietly. "I'm going to do some more tonging."

"No!"

She started at the forcefulness of his tone and turned to look at him. His expression was brooding and his mouth was grim. "I'll tong. And I won't tell you what to do. Do the culling or eat your chicken or whatever you want. Suit yourself." He strode past her, and Kate stared after him, appalled at the damage she'd done. She hadn't meant to hurt him — the words had just slipped out before she could think.

Jim tackled the tonging with the energy of three men, maintaining a brutal pace that Kate knew was serving as an outlet for his pain. He worked as though the devil himself were on his back, moving from the prow to the work table, dumping load after load of oysters.

Kate stood watching him from the cabin, aching with the need to comfort him in some way. Finally she pushed open the door and walked hesitantly to his side. "I don't have any excuse for what I said," she began. "It was just stupidity. I treated you like an outsider. But I truly didn't mean to hurt you. I've lost friends on the bay, and I pray every time Buck goes out that he'll return safely. All I can say is I'm sorry."

He stopped and leaned on the tongs, the ferocity gradually fading from his face. "It happened a long time ago," he said quietly. "I didn't mean to act like such an ogre. I hope I didn't lower your opinion of me . . . if it's possible for me to go any lower."

She smiled and shook her head. "Why don't we eat that chicken now before we turn back?"

"All right."

They sat back down at the table and, though Jim made small talk, Kate realized he was deliberately avoiding any mention of tonging or his family. There was now a polite distance between them. It was as though he had withdrawn into himself, and she was talking to his shadow.

It came as a surprise when he suddenly said, "If I'm not being overbearing, would you consider having dinner with me tomorrow night?" Her expression must have reflected surprise, because he added wryly, "I promise not to cut your meat for you."

She had a strong suspicion that if she accepted his invitation she was liable to find herself in his arms again. That was a prospect she wasn't sure she could handle. His touch summoned up primitive responses that went far beyond anything she'd experienced before. Half of her thirsted for the pleasure he'd awakened in her, and the other half warned her that she'd better prepare herself to walk away with a broken heart when it was over.

"I want to pay my own way," she said at last, trying to strike a compromise with her warring emotions. If she maintained her independence, she might be able to retain some control over the situation.

Jim quirked one eyebrow and looked at

her dourly. "Are we going to fight over this, Miss Flannery?"

"All right, Mr. Carlisle," she said, giving in with a smile, "you may pay, but it's Captain Flannery to you."

"Aye, aye, Captain," he said softly, and his eyes grew warmer. He grinned at her, and Kate felt heat suffuse her body. When he relaxed his guard there was a boyish half-smile playing on his lips, as though they were sharing some secret, and his hazel eyes gleamed with self-assured charm. A man like Jim could twist a woman around his finger with no effort, she thought regretfully.

To break the mood, she asked flippantly, "Well, what did you bring for dessert today?"

"Is that all you think of, your stomach?" he demanded.

"According to you, my waking thoughts are entirely consumed with visions of junk food. I'm only living up to my image."

He gave a noncommittal grunt and shot her a wry glance. "It just so happens that I brought cake."

"Chocolate?" she asked hopefully.

"Chocolate." He stood up and brought over two pieces of chocolate cake wrapped on paper plates. He handed one to Kate. "I trust that saves me from walking the plank today, Captain?"

"Definitely. In fact, you deserve a promotion. How about First Mate? You get to flog all the insubordinates."

"Such an attractive job description. How can I refuse?"

"I thought that might appeal to you. And be sure to quell any and all mutinies."

"Hell, I'll even flog the oysters if you say so, Captain."

Kate felt the corners of her mouth turn up irresistibly, then her laughter bubbled over.

"Ah, Captain Kate," Jim said with mock seriousness, his eyes gleaming, "this sense of humor isn't good for your image."

Kate flashed him a wide grin. "Then maybe it's time I changed my image."

Kate rose and carried both plates to the trash basket. But when she turned around she found Jim standing in front of her, and she backed up until she was against the small counter. Suddenly she was intensely aware of his height and the way his black jacket clung to his tapered waist. He stepped closer, and Kate drew in her breath as his gaze swept her face. Those hazel eyes were her undoing — they seemed to start little fires deep within her, fires that reminded her that she was a woman after all, and he was a man.

He was standing only a foot away from her now, and she could feel her heart pounding against her ribs. She seemed to be trembling all over, and either the cabin had shrunk alarmingly or she'd suddenly mushroomed in size.

"You have icing on your mouth," he said softly. She closed her eyes against the magnetic force of his nearness, and then she felt one strong finger brushing her lips. The fires inside flamed.

The gentle pressure of his finger ceased, and she held her breath, waiting, knowing there was more to come. *Stop him now,* a little voice inside her warned, *before it's too late.* But she was unable to move, afraid of the power of his touch, yet craving it.

His lips came down on hers with bruising force, as though all restraint had given way. His fingers caught her hair and cradled her head as her neck bent back beneath his onslaught. Raising his mouth fractionally, he muttered her name against her lips, and then his tongue sought entrance, tasting her lips and exploring the moist treasure beyond.

The world had suddenly spun nearer the sun, and the heat was melting her bones. The singing in her blood was carrying his name to her brain, her eyes, her heart. She'd never felt such raw desire. It threatened to tear her apart with its intensity.

Jim moved his mouth to her throat, his teeth teasing her relentlessly. Dimly she realized that she was on the brink of surrendering. "Jim," she whispered raggedly, "I can't fight this."

He pressed his mouth against her throat, and she felt his kiss change from passionate to gentle. Very slowly he pulled away, his hands trailing over her cheeks and mouth with a light touch. He lowered his arms to his sides, and Kate leaned heavily against the sink.

"I don't want you to fight me, Kate," he said softly, almost in a whisper. "I won't do anything you aren't ready for. Trust me."

"I'm trying," she said shakily.

"I know you are, sweetheart. I know you are." His mouth curved in a reassuring smile.

The air in the cabin still seemed charged with electricity, and Kate realized her fingers were laced tightly in front of her.

"We'd better start back," she said quietly.

He nodded and moved toward the cabin door. Kate was still leaning against the counter when he turned to face her. "I'm not the enemy, Kate," he said quietly. "Remember that."

But you are, she said to herself, watching him walk onto the deck. *You're the enemy because you make me feel vulnerable.*

After he'd cleared the deck, he stood silently near the cabin, his eyes riveted on the shoreline, hands clenched on the side of the boat. Kate ventured out to start the engine and begin the trip back. Jim didn't look at her all the way home, and she finally relaxed, realizing he was deliberately giving her breathing space.

Watching his brows knit in thought and his eyes intent on the bay, Kate wondered if he were caught up again in reliving his father's death. She had been too young when her parents died to experience the deep pain Jim must have felt. She'd seen other families on Tilghman Island who'd lost a waterman to the bay, and she'd felt some of the grief they bore.

Jim's father must have been a strong man to turn his back on the Carlisle fortune for the hard life of the Chesapeake. And what about the son? Was he as strong? Kate frowned. Jim wasn't a waterman. He'd made his own choice, and it had been Carlisle Refineries. That was the sharp line dividing them.

There were always choices to be made, and sometimes the wrong one made life painful. Her mistake had been Jeffrey. He'd had no love — not even respect — for the bay. And he'd had none for Kate, though they'd both believed differently in the beginning. He'd come to her empty-hearted, with nothing to give and wanting only to take.

They were almost to the buyer's wharf. Kate wrenched her thoughts back to the present and concentrated on docking the boat. When the oysters were weighed and she had collected the money, she approached Jim hesitantly. "Here's your pay," she said, holding out the bills.

"Thank you," he said quietly, pocketing them. "I'll see you tomorrow night. I'll pick you up around six."

That night Kate made a pot of tea and stretched out on the couch, determined to make some headway with her journals. Dinner had been a makeshift affair of a left-over pork chop and applesauce. She sipped some tea, covered her legs with a warm afghan, and opened the first journal.

She groaned when she heard a knock on the door. Buck's friends were always checking in to see if she was okay or needed anything. Though she appreciated their concern, she wanted to be alone that night. She left the warm couch and pushed aside the curtain at the door before opening it. "Mary, come on in. You look like you're freezing."

"Thanks, Kate." The young woman smiled and hurried inside, rubbing her hands together. "If I'd known it was going to get this cold out tonight, I would have put on more than a sweater."

"Here, sit down. I'll get you some tea."

"Don't go to any trouble."

"It's no trouble," Kate said, smiling. "I have some made already."

Mary settled herself at the kitchen table and pushed her hair back from her face. After Kate had set two cups on the table and sat down, she smiled warmly at her friend. "How are Frank and the kids getting along?"

"Okay," Mary said. "The dredging's been pretty good, and the kids are doing all right in school. It's been a real shocker to have both of them away from home during the day. Sometimes I find myself fixing lunch for them when they're gone."

"Be grateful for the free time. Wasn't it just a few years ago that you said you were a prisoner of your house, surrounded by diapers and toys?"

Mary nodded, reminiscent light touching her eyes. She was a slightly chubby woman with short, light brown hair that bordered on being frizzy. With her round face and ready smile she looked almost elfin.

Mary lowered her voice to a conspiratorial tone, though they were alone except for Fudge. "Frank says a man's been going tonging with you. Is it true? Was that his Porsche that followed you home last night?"

Kate laughed at the eager curiosity on Mary's face. "Yes, and yes again."

"That's terrific!" Mary squealed in genuine delight. "It's about time you started seeing someone, Kate. Now who is he and what's he like? He must be rich to own a Porsche. At least that's what Frank says. He said he didn't think he was from around here either."

"Whoa." Kate laughed. "Slow down a minute, and I'll tell you. No, he isn't from around here. His name's Jim Carlisle, and he's —"

"Jim Carlisle!" Mary's eyes widened. "He's not one of *the* Carlisles, is he?"

"That's right. He's a petroleum engineer at Carlisle Refineries. Right now he's on vacation, so he's doing some tonging to keep busy." She refrained from mentioning anything about Jim's father, feeling it was too personal and hoping Mary wouldn't pry.

"You mean he just showed up one day looking for tonging work?"

"Well, not exactly." Kate hesitated, then said, "He read my letter to the editor and came around to . . . well . . . straighten me out."

"You're kidding!" Mary exploded in peals of laughter. "He didn't! That must have been some meeting." When Kate confirmed it with a nod, Mary laughed harder. "Well, it looks like you two ironed out your differences," she added with a grin.

"A little."

"Jim Carlisle," Mary repeated thoughtfully. "Now which one is he? I guess he'd have to be the nephew. Louise Carlisle Andrews doesn't have any children of her own." She seemed not to notice Kate's piqued curiosity and went on with her ruminations. "Let's see now." Mary's face took on the look of a woman sifting through a recipe file. "I remember reading something about him in the paper a while back. Now what was it?" Suddenly she frowned in remembrance and glanced at Kate. "It was his wedding."

Kate felt a momentary jolt, but kept her features relaxed. "Are you sure?"

Mary nodded. "It was on the society page, a big picture and everything. Well, never mind. He must be divorced."

Kate nodded with a weak smile, but inside was shaking. She could hardly concentrate on the rest of the conversation. It was only later when she sat alone with the empty teacups in front of her that she began to recover from the numbness that had settled over her at Mary's words. No, she was sure Jim wasn't divorced. She remembered making a feeble joke about it once, and he'd told her no. Mary couldn't be right. He couldn't be married. Maybe he was a widower.

But the worry gnawed at her all night long. If there'd been a death, Mary probably would have read that too. She must be mistaken. It must have been another Carlisle.

chapter

4

Kate flung her coat on a kitchen chair and put on a pot of water for coffee, then stared broodingly out the window until the water came to a boil. While the water dripped methodically through the fresh grounds, she leaned against the window, watching two blackbirds pick through the fallow cornfield next to the house. Beyond the field stretched the bay, bare trees clustered near the bank. Across the field she could see Mary hanging her wash on the line.

It was a crisp, cold Saturday, the kind of November day when the watermen used to gather in the house years ago when Kate was a little girl. They'd come one by one on a Saturday, bringing a little cider or a bit of coffeecake, maybe some bread baked by their wives. Buck would put on the coffeepot and sit down with them at the kitchen table. Kate would curl up in her little chair by the warm stove, listening to the tales the men told while they hunched over their steaming mugs. The stories they told were funny or sad, but all were poignant, and they made her believe in a reality that was larger than life.

Maybe that was what was wrong with her, Kate thought. She'd listened to those stories of men and women who'd been as grand and beautiful as the Chesapeake, and she'd believed them all. She'd learned to expect too much of life, to believe that those stories told around the kitchen table were true. But they weren't. They were exaggerations of life, gallant portraits that flattered their subjects.

She sank down at the table and sipped the coffee without tasting it. Jim was coming that night to take her out to dinner, but she wasn't going to be there waiting for him.

Kate had gone to the newspaper office that morning and asked for permission to search their files in the morgue. She'd taken out the file on the Carlisles and had read about the big society wedding of James Carlisle and Leora Mason.

In the picture Jim had been smiling, his boyish charm evident even in grainy black and white. Leora Mason had been a radiant bride, her head resting on Jim's chest just below his chin. Her veil framed her heart-shaped face, and she held a bouquet of roses. The article said they would be honeymooning in California. According to the write-up, Leora was a prominent debutante, her father president of a major local wholesale oil supplier, her mother head of umpteen charities and chairwoman of the Belles Dames Ball.

Kate had gone over the possibilities again. Jim might be divorced. But she remembered he'd said, *"No, not a divorce."*

Had Leora died? Surely a subsequent newspaper article would have reported her death, but Kate had searched the Carlisle file and found no mention of it.

You're running scared, Kate, an inner voice taunted her. *You've met a man who knocks the socks off your size-seven feet, and you can't handle it.*

"That's not true," she protested fiercely. And she kept repeating that until she almost believed it.

Her anger mounted as the afternoon wore on. Jim had used her. He was just like Jeffrey, only more compelling. She was physically attracted to him and nothing more. To pretend otherwise was to imagine the impossible. She would never have a relationship with a man like Jim. Whatever had begun was over.

Too restless to work, Kate drove to the

nursing home to visit Buck, hoping that would take her mind off everything. As usual, he was eager to complain about the home. Kate listened patiently for the first ten minutes. They were sitting in the sun room, Buck with his cast stretched out in front of him, his thick white hair as unruly as ever, as though the wind on the bay had blown it into permanent disarray. His face was full and rosy-cheeked, the blue eyes still crackling with life, though the thick brows over them had long ago turned snowy. "The food in this place is unfit for human consumption," Buck rasped. "Kate, I'd give my best set of tongs for one of our Friday night croquettes."

"Buck, you know as well as I do that those croquettes always give you indigestion," she reminded him gently. "Neither of us is exactly chef material. Besides, you look like you've gained a pound or two on this cooking."

"It just looks that way," he grumbled. "They won't let me have any beer in here anyway."

"From what I hear at the docks, your buddies are keeping you pretty well supplied on the sly," she chided him.

"So you heard about that, did you?" he said, grinning. He lowered his voice gleefully. "Kate, you should have seen that night nurse when she saw five watermen climbing back over the fence the other night. She ran into my room demanding to know what they were doing sneaking in here. I told her they were consulting doctors. I thought she was going to have a fit." He chuckled at the memory, then turned his penetrating blue eyes on her. "And what about you, Kate?" he asked mischievously. "I hear you haven't been tonging alone."

"And I suppose your sources told you all about that."

"That they did. A Carlisle, eh? From what I hear he does a pretty fair amount of work."

"He pulls his share," she admitted grudgingly.

Buck waited, then said, "You don't get along very well with this Mr. Carlisle?"

"We have our differences," she said quietly. One of them being his wife, she thought to herself.

"No chance of something serious developing?" he pressed.

She shook her head adamantly. "He's not right for me, Buck."

He leaned back in his chair and shook his head, his disappointment evident. "I'd hoped he would be, Katie."

"Now stop trying to match me up with

every eligible bachelor who comes along," she said, making her voice light. "It won't work."

"It's worth a try," he defended himself. "You need someone, Kate. I miss my Kathryn so much sometimes. I wish you'd known her better, Katie. You were so little when she died. A fine woman she was. Now that was a marriage. Oh, we had our fights. Some of them were loud enough to carry across the bay." He chuckled. "But that was part of it. You scrap and you make up, and all the time you know you've got something you want to go on forever." His face sobered, and he added, "Well, it didn't go on forever for me, but I want you to have something that good, Katie. Not like that idiot Jeffrey."

"Jeffrey's not an idiot." She sighed, thinking of a far worse name for him.

Buck shook his head. "Any man who'd give you up is an idiot, Katie." She had to smile at the way he said it, as though it were a truth that any fool could recognize.

"Well, I don't want another man, Buck, so you and your cronies can give up trying."

Buck's eyes lit up devilishly. "Red told me how he sent that Jim Carlisle over to your boat without telling him you was a girl. Bet that was something."

Kate pursed her lips in mock sternness. "I won't put up with any more shenanigans from you or Red."

"I bet you two had the row of the century when you found out who he was." He chortled, openly daring her to tell him the story.

"I didn't discover who he was until the end of the day," she retorted firmly. With a frown she added, "Though we did bicker some the next day."

"The next day?" Buck's bushy eyebrows rose. "So he came back for more, eh, Katie?"

"The man's obviously a masochist," she snapped. "Now let's get off the subject of Jim Carlisle."

"Anything you say, Kate." But there was a sparkle in his eyes that belied his solemn tone. *The old devil,* she thought with a hidden smile. For all Buck's teasing, Kate was secure in the knowledge that he loved her more than anything else in his life and would protect her to the death. She had nearly had to restrain him after Jeffrey had left her. And now Jim. Well, if Jim Carlisle insisted on pushing her after tonight, she would consider turning Buck on him. *Then see if you think watermen are something to toy with,* she thought coldly.

At six o'clock Kate walked down to the

edge of the bay with Fudge. She'd left the car in the driveway and the door locked. She planned to let Jim figure out for himself that she didn't want to see him. Still, she cursed her cowardice for not staying inside the house or, better yet, facing him. But if he had only been playing a game with her, she didn't want to have to see him again.

Fudge was enjoying a romp on the bank, his head or a paw plunging in and out of burrows and barking in excitement as the water rippled around his feet. It was dark already, and Kate had to pick her way carefully to avoid tripping over exposed tree roots.

It was probably about six-thirty by now, she figured. Hopefully Jim had realized that she was standing him up and had left. She ventured closer to the shoreline, listening to the lap of water against the coarse mixture of sand and mud. The bay had a rhythm of its own, a rocking set up in part by the ship traffic that used it as a watery highway. Tankers and freighters rode up the channel toward Wilmington, Delaware, and other ports. The bay was a life-giving artery.

It must be closer to seven by now. Kate shivered involuntarily as the damp cold penetrated her windbreaker. Surely she could go back. Fudge was barking again, this time at a raccoon or possum that had been drawn to the water. Kate hugged her arms to herself.

"So this is where you're hiding."

She jumped and spun around, her eyes wide with shock. "Wh-what are you doing here?" she cried in a shaky voice.

"I thought we had a dinner date."

"How did you find me?" she demanded, her heart pounding at the start he'd given her.

"I'm not in the habit of scouring the countryside for my dinner dates, but I heard Fudge barking," Jim explained patiently, a twinge of sarcasm in his voice. "I see you need to either buy a watch or teach that dog of yours to tell time."

"I can tell time perfectly well," she replied icily, watching as his eyebrows rose in mockery. He looked especially attractive tonight, she thought, dressed in gray pants that hugged his slim hips and a black pullover sweater. He'd slung his jacket casually over his shoulder and was watching her through eyes grown suddenly flinty in the pale moonlight.

"Are you trying to tell me you aren't keeping our date?" he asked.

"That's right."

As if in response to a sorcerer's spell, the

moonlight shone suddenly on his chiseled features, and Kate chided herself for the way her pulse raced.

"And your peculiarly individual way of telling me was to hide down here by the water? Haven't you heard of that marvelous new invention called the telephone?" Jim demanded.

It suddenly struck her that he thought her actions childish, and, truthfully, she was having difficulty justifying them herself. "Well, now you know," she ground out through clenched teeth.

"Of course. That explains everything," he said, a sharp edge to his voice that hinted at his rising temper. Kate felt her own anger increasing and had to remind herself sharply that he wasn't worth her fury.

When she said nothing, he strode toward her and put his hands on her shoulders, turning her to the light so he could see her face. Kate's knees grew weak and her pulse raced even faster under his touch. "Now how about telling me what this is all about?" he said impatiently.

"I told you — I don't want to go to dinner with you."

"That really explains everything," he repeated sarcastically. "Is this twenty questions? Why don't you want to go to dinner with me? Are you too tired — is that it?"

"No." She shook her head angrily, avoiding his eyes.

His grip tightened, and she felt she had to say something or be swamped with a longing she couldn't afford to feel. His touch was conjuring up images of his hands and lips on her, which brought heated anticipation to every nerve ending. "I wouldn't want to deprive your wife of your company at dinner tonight," she said finally.

Immediately the strong fingers released her. He lifted his hands from her shoulders, suspending them in midair a moment as if he wanted to touch her, then, as if with supreme effort, he lowered them to his side and stared at her in the moonlight. "And how did you find out about my wife?" he asked coldly, a hard expression on his face that almost frightened her.

She felt miserable. She realized now she'd hoped he would deny her accusation. But he hadn't. "A friend of mine remembered reading about the wedding in the newspaper," she explained calmly, surprised that she could keep her voice so steady. "I checked on it." She closed her eyes briefly against his sardonic expression. "And I discovered she was right. There was no mention of a divorce," she added coolly.

"Nor of a death?" His voice was steel-coated ice.

"No," she whispered hoarsely.

There was a long, tense silence, then Jim's voice broke the stillness, his words low and controlled, but apparently spoken with difficulty. "Leora was killed in a car accident in California last year."

Kate's mouth worked soundlessly as her stomach twisted into a painful knot. She hadn't even given him a chance; she'd simply accused him and in the process she'd wounded him again. Why did she hurt him like this without thinking? It was almost as though she were looking for an excuse to push him out of her life.

Her eyes filled with tears, but she held her head up. "I'm so sorry. I'm not usually this callous and stupid."

"You had no way of knowing. We were able to keep it out of the papers here."

The silence grew heavy between them, and Kate began to shiver, partly from cold and partly from a deeply buried fear that she'd succeeded in alienating him permanently. He made no move toward her, and she stared down at the ground, feeling miserable and alone.

"Why don't we go eat?" he asked softly. Kate stared up at him in surprise. "I assume you haven't lost your appetite."

The old teasing note was back in his voice, and Kate smiled in response. "I'd like that," she said simply.

They started back toward the house, Fudge running ahead of them, his tongue lolling out in the cold air. Kate let him inside, then offered Jim coffee while she brushed her hair and put on some lipstick. He was looking out her kitchen window when she returned, his hazel eyes focused on something distant. Kate stood watching him silently for a moment, wondering about Leora and the effect her death had had on him. She didn't think she'd ever forget the raw pain on his face in the dim moonlight when he'd told her about Leora.

He turned and smiled at her. "You look great. Ready?"

The restaurant was on the Eastern Shore, a small, intimate place, totally unpretentious. Long picnic tables were covered with red-checked cloths and a flickering candle in a red glass holder cast silvery shadows on their faces. The waiter brought them each a beer and piles of fried oysters, crab cakes, and clams. They ate the succulent meal with coleslaw, French fries, and corn bread, and Kate felt thoroughly satiated when they looked at each other over their empty plates and smiled.

"Did you ever run a trotline for crabs?" Kate asked as they pushed their plates away.

"Of course," Jim replied. "All watermen go crabbing in the summer, don't they?"

"Without a doubt," she answered blithely. "I think I liked that even more than oystering. At least it was warmer. Buck and I would get up early and pack a thermos of coffee and some donuts, then set off about sunrise. Sometimes, if the carnival was in town, we'd go there at night. I'd get so excited." She laughed, remembering. "And I always wanted to go on the Ferris wheel — at least until we got in line," she added wryly. "Then I'd chicken out. But, still, summer here was always so . . ." She stopped, fishing for the right word.

"Exciting?" Jim suggested.

"Yes, that's it." She looked at him, then sobered. "Winter can be exciting too, but in a different way. Mostly it's hard work."

"And dangerous." She was afraid to say it, but she could tell the thought was preying on his mind.

"I used to go oystering with my father every winter," he said, his voice low and controlled, but she caught the thread of grief it held. "Our boat was the *Black Sheep*."

Kate widened her eyes. When Jim glanced at her wryly, she said, "Did his family really consider him a black sheep just because he was a waterman?"

Jim nodded. "They turned their backs on him once he'd decided to live his life on the bay. He couldn't stand the high-powered lifestyle of an oil executive." Jim shrugged. "All choices demand a sacrifice of some kind; he made the one he could live with. But it was a short life." There was a long silence while Jim stared down at the table, frowning. Kate waited.

"I left for college one September," he said at last. "It was cold that fall and rainy. I had two, maybe three letters from my father by November when the oyster season started. Then he was too busy to write. The phone call came one icy day early in December. He'd been out alone as usual. Nobody knows what really happened. Maybe he was checking something in the back of the boat. Whatever the reason, he fell overboard. You know what that means for an oysterman."

A shudder ran through Kate. She knew all too well what it meant. He didn't have a chance. He might as well cling to an anchor. "The bay claims its own," she murmured softly, her eyes filling with tears. She caught

Jim staring at her intently and flushed. "I'm sorry. It just came to mind."

"No, you're right." The intensity in his voice riveted her. "That's exactly how I felt. I took that boat out one night and set fire to it. I watched it go up in flames like a funeral pyre. After that, I felt that I'd truly laid my father to rest." His eyes seemed to burn into her. "No one understood. They all said I'd gone crazy with grief."

"I understand," she said quietly.

"Yes, I think you do," he said slowly. "It's more than a way of life, isn't it?"

Kate nodded. "It *is* life, Jim."

"That's it." A gentle smile spread over his face. "Yes, Kate, that's it."

It was a magical moment, one in which she felt totally as one with him. It was something she'd felt previously only alone on the water, never with another person. Instinctively she knew that Jim represented a danger to her — not the danger found on the bay but a threat of a different kind.

Injecting a lightness into her tone that she didn't feel, she said, "It looks like they're clearing off the tables. Maybe we should go before we get put out with the cat."

Jim regarded her thoughtfully, and she knew she hadn't fooled him. But he let it pass. "Okay," he said quietly. "How about going to my apartment for a nightcap? I guarantee the butler won't disturb us."

Panic rose in Kate's throat. "I don't know," she murmured. "I really should get home."

They'd stood up to leave, and now Jim took her arm, turning her to face him. She felt her heart pounding. "Such a little coward," he said wryly. "You brave the bay alone, and you face life unafraid, but you're too chicken to come to my apartment."

He was right; she couldn't deny the accusation. The bay didn't scare her half as much as he did.

"Take a chance, Kate," he said. "Don't run away."

"All right," she said at last with a shaky smile. "One ticket for the Ferris wheel."

"I can't promise you that much," he said with a grin as he led her outside, "but I do have a decent bottle of amaretto."

His apartment was a pleasant surprise. "Early American clutter," he called it.

Kate wandered around the spacious living room in wonder, going from bookshelves to coffee table to desk. Everywhere there were momentos and collectibles, as though Jim's life was so full that he never had time to put anything in its proper place, never hid anything from view. Strewn on every shelf of the bookcase were rocks from his collection, an agate beside Tolstoy, a large piece of amethyst in front of Jane Austen.

Kate shook her head as all the impressions hit her at once. It was almost too much to assimilate. The coffee table was covered with art books that Jim scooped aside when he set down two glasses of amber liquid. Kate sat down on the plush brown couch and sipped from a glass, enjoying the sweet almond taste. The living room was very comfortable. The carpeting was soft beige, and there were two other chairs with a brown-and-white-checked upholstery that complemented the couch. But it wasn't the furniture that caught her attention. It was the ambience, if that was the word to describe it.

When Kate looked at Jim, sitting in the chair opposite her, he was grinning. "Your tastes are certainly eclectic," she commented.

"My aunt calls it messy." He laughed. "You're more diplomatic. A lot of the things were my father's — the jade and some of the shells. I've collected the rocks myself, mostly on field trips. The watercolors," he said, gesturing toward the walls, "I picked up in shops here and there. And the dirty

96

breakfast dishes are a recent acquisition." He nodded toward the kitchen.

Kate smiled, but didn't say anything. A moment later Jim said, "Ah, very good! Most women immediately volunteer to do the dishes for me. A female reaction I've never understood. I dirtied them so I should clean them."

Kate flushed and put down her glass. "You're a trifle more liberated than most men. Besides that, I assumed Jeeves would do them for you."

Jim laughed, a rich, contagious sound that filled Kate with as much warmth as the amaretto. "As I mentioned before, Jeeves has the evening off."

"Lucky Jeeves." She smiled. "You're a generous employer."

"Come here," he said softly, rising and coming toward her.

Kate stood up nervously and Jim led her to the window. "Now this is my view," he said in mock seriousness. She looked down on an apartment parking lot filled with cars and beyond them the city street. "I want you to admire the magnificent pavement," Jim added wryly, "and the artistic way the traffic lights blink different colors. And of course all the cars zipping by. The occasional blast of a horn adds atmosphere."

"Did you do the landscaping yourself?" she replied going along with his game.

"The apartment came complete. Now when I take you home to your view of the bay and fields and wild geese, you can feel sorry for yourself because you don't have a parking lot to look out over."

"I'll try to overcome my envy," she said with mock seriousness.

Jim smiled down at her as his arm went around her waist. Kate found herself unable to look away, and she let him draw her closer, longing to touch him, to feel his silky hair beneath her fingers and those hard muscles of his back. But she held herself in check, acquiescing only slightly to the pressure of his hand on her waist.

Just then the phone rang.

"Where's Jeeves when we need him?" Jim muttered with a sigh.

Kate remained by the window as he picked up the receiver. From the conversation she gathered that it was his aunt. "I'll probably see you Sunday," he concluded. "No, Louise. Thank you, but I don't think I'll be over for Thanksgiving. I appreciate the invitation. All right. Good-bye."

He put down the phone and turned to Kate. "Now where were we?"

He was standing in front of her almost

before she realized it. Like a graceful animal, he moved with fluid ease. One strong hand cupped her chin, and Kate held her breath when she saw the smoldering desire in his eyes. He wanted her, and he was making no secret of it.

Her blood pounded in her ears like the ocean tide, a timeless rhythm. His thumb caressed her lower lip, making her sigh against the sensual pressure. She waited for his kiss like a wanderer lost on the desert thirsting for a drink of water.

Her mouth parted eagerly as his descended on hers, and she was caught in a vortex of pleasure. His arms went around her, pulling her tightly against him, making her vividly aware of his firm thighs. She'd seen butterflies caught in spider webs, struggling futilely against silken threads that held them captive more effectively than steel bands. That's what she was — captive of a desire so sweet that she was incapable of breaking free.

His fingers played at the nape of her neck, sending heated pulses down her back. His hands and mouth were telling her he wanted her, and Kate felt herself melting closer against him.

"Jim."

She didn't even realize she'd said his

name until he drew back to look down into her face.

She wasn't ready to let go completely and entrust herself to him. Some vestige of her sanity must have realized that and said his name, calling them both from a growing passion.

He traced a line down her cheek with his finger. "It won't always end like this, Kate," he promised her softly. "We both know it. I'll have you one day."

He went to get her coat, and Kate leaned weakly against the windowsill. He'd released her from the silken bonds this time, but he was still in pursuit. What frightened her was that her traitorous body was looking forward to the capture.

He was quiet on the ride to her house. Kate finally broke the silence. "Are you spending Thanksgiving with your mother?" she asked tentatively, remembering how he'd turned down his aunt's invitation.

He shook his head. "My mother remarried and is living in Phoenix."

"Oh. Since you aren't going to your aunt's, I assumed you had other plans."

Jim grimaced in the dim light of the car. "Actually I prefer solitude to my Aunt Louise's house at Thanksgiving. She makes it a social affair rather than family, and every name on the social register is invited. Very ta-ta. I'd prefer to dine alone with Jeeves," he added, his eyes twinkling.

"I see." After a moment of silence, Kate ventured, "You could have Thanksgiving with Buck and me, if you want."

She heard the smile in his voice. "Turkey croquettes?"

"Not until at least six days after Thanksgiving," she promised with a laugh. "Buck and I usually manage to truss up the turkey ourselves, and he gets a home-cured ham from friends. There's more than enough food."

"It sounds great. I'd like to come."

The white Porsche turned into Kate's driveway, and Fudge leaped up from the porch as the headlights swung over him. Jim got out and walked Kate to the door. She felt reluctant to say good night. He unlocked the door, then stood leaning against its frame, staring down at her. The pale moonlight illuminated his face, and Kate swallowed when she caught his spellbinding smile. Slowly his head bent toward hers. She stood mesmerized. One hand tilted her chin up toward him. She closed her eyes with a shudder as his face blocked her vision, and then he was kissing her, not hard and demanding but gently and with great tenderness. It wasn't what she'd expected, and she found herself wanting more. Her hand stole around his neck to hold him closer.

The kiss deepened, and Kate's mouth parted for him. But when his hand slid down her back to pull her tighter against him, she stiffened, sensing that the tender trap was about to close over her. Slowly he released her. She was breathing hard, staring back at him, and she knew her hesitation was obvious. "I guess I'm just a coward after all," she whispered.

Jim shook his head. "You were hurt once, Kate, and you're afraid of it happening again." He regarded her solemnly. "I can't promise you'll never be hurt again. There's pain enough in the world for everyone. But there's joy, too, Kate, and you're shielding yourself from both of them. Take a chance on life, Captain."

She breathed deeply, remembering the Ferris wheel and how she used to run away.

"Remember what your uncle said the other day about penny candy?" he reminded her. She felt her face coloring as the words came back vividly. Jim smiled and pulled a small bag from his jacket pocket. "Here. I'll collect on this another time."

He placed a quick kiss on her cheek and

then strode lithely to his car. Kate went inside the house, Fudge trailing behind, and stood at the window until the Porsche disappeared into the night. Slowly she uncurled her fingers from the bag and opened it. Penny candy, a whole bag of it. Heat washed over her as she imagined him collecting on it.

Mary came over the next afternoon, and Kate put on a pot of tea. They were sitting in the kitchen eating cookies, Mary rattling on about the kids playing and Frank working on the car when they heard a car pull up in the driveway. Mary glanced out the window and turned to Kate excitedly. "It's him!" she exclaimed.

"Who?"

"Jim Carlisle! You didn't tell me he was coming today."

"Because I didn't know." Kate ran her fingers through her hair and tucked her red plaid flannel shirt into her jeans.

She didn't get up from the table until Jim knocked on the door, then tried to appear nonchalant while Mary looked on with obvious interest.

"I didn't expect you," Kate blurted out as soon as she let him in.

"Am I intruding?" he asked at once,

glancing past her to Mary.

Kate shook her head. "Jim Carlisle, this is my neighbor Mary Peterson."

Mary stood up with a bright smile and shook the hand Jim offered. "Glad to meet you, Jim."

"The pleasure's mine."

After a moment of awkward silence, Mary said, "Well, I should be getting back home. It's about time for the kids' lunch. Nice meeting you, Jim." She gave Kate a conspiratorial wink on her way out, and Kate managed a half-hearted smile in return.

"I see I caught you in the middle of lunch," Jim said with a wry glance toward the table where the half-empty plate of cookies sat. He held out a brown sack. "Still hungry?"

Kate peered into the bag, then exclaimed delightedly, "Chinese! Terrific! I haven't had any in ages."

She put a record on the stereo in the living room, and they sat at the kitchen table eating Chinese food and drinking hot tea. The sky was gray and heavy clouds hung low over the bay, but Kate felt warm and safe inside the house with Jim.

A comfortable silence stretched between them as they ate. Finally sated, they both sat back in their chairs. "Thanks," Kate said.

"That was delicious. Would you like a piece of candy for dessert?" She picked up the bag from the counter and held it out with a mischievous smile.

"Is that an invitation?"

She was about to say yes, but Fudge chose that moment to bark at the door. Kate got up to let him in, growing warmer as she felt Jim's eyes on her. "Fudge!" The dog zipped past her, his coat splattered with dark patches. Kate ran after him.

Jim followed, and the three of them played a ridiculous game of tag in the living room, Fudge eluding them as he ran behind the couch. Jim and Kate circled in from opposite sides. But just when Kate thought they had Fudge cornered, he dashed between her legs, sending Kate sprawling onto the floor.

"I think we ought to explain the rules of this game to him," Jim said, laughing as he helped Kate to her feet.

Fudge barked playfully from the kitchen doorway, and they began to advance on him again. The dog knelt on his front legs, tail waving jauntily in the air. With all the grace of two elephants on roller skates, Jim and Kate leaped at him, only to land on the floor in a tangled heap as Fudge jumped backwards. Kate's legs were entwined with

Jim's, and she suddenly realized she was lying on top of him. "Best game of tag I ever played," he growled huskily, grinning up at her. Kate propped herself up, laughing, and Fudge dashed over and licked their faces enthusiastically. Jim serenaded the dog with a baritone chorus of "Gimme a Little Kiss" while Kate erupted into uncontrollable giggles.

Jim helped her half-drag and half-carry a protesting Fudge down the basement steps to the shower. "Look at you!" Kate chided him. "There's oil on your coat!"

"I assure you it's not a Carlisle Refinery spill," Jim interjected quickly.

"You're off the hook this time," she told him with mock severity. "Frank was working on his car, and it looks like Fudge decided to help."

"I've never bathed a mechanic before," Jim said as Kate turned on the shower.

The canine mechanic planted all four paws firmly, making it clear he was only just tolerating the bath. Together, Jim and Kate lathered him with a bar of soap, struggling to hold him still. Kate turned on the shower again, and they began rinsing off the retriever's coat.

As if suddenly losing patience with the whole process, Fudge made a leap for freedom. Kate shrieked as he escaped them. Grabbing for him, Kate slid on a piece of soap and made a four-point landing on her backside directly under the shower spray. She gurgled a few unintelligible words before Jim managed to turn off the shower.

"That dog is demonic!" Kate fumed, rising slowly to her feet, water pouring from her in little rivulets. She glared at Fudge, who had retreated to safety under the stairs. He promptly shook the water from his coat, sending droplets flying across the room, then trotted up the stairs as if all was finally right with the world.

Kate gave one last irritated groan and turned to Jim, who regarded her with his hands on his hips, obviously trying to suppress a grin.

"So you think it's funny, do you?" Kate said, hiding her own smile. She began to advance on him menacingly, and Jim backed away.

"Now all we have to do is dry you off and find your flea collar," Jim teased her, a grin splitting his face.

"You're going to regret that remark, Jim Carlisle," she threatened him, chasing him around the basement, both of them laughing now.

She cornered him near the sump pump

and eyed him suspiciously. "You were awfully easy to catch."

"Maybe I wanted to be caught."

Suddenly the game became serious. They both stood motionless.

"You're pretty sexy for a lady who's got soap bubbles on her nose," he said, reaching out to touch her there lightly.

Flames of desire flared inside Kate as his fingers feathered down her nose and over her lips. He stroked her throat with incredible tenderness, making her breath catch when she realized that his hand was trembling.

She was overcome with a need to touch him, and she tentatively brought her fingers to his face. His skin was damp and warm, and, as she stepped closer, she caught the faint smell of musk. She let her hands rove over his high cheekbones and the hollows beneath. His mouth opened slightly as her fingers traced his lips, and he began kissing her fingers one by one. "Kate," he murmured.

Giving her instincts free rein, she tangled her hands in his hair, letting the coarse strands glide over her palms. He fastened his mouth on the side of her neck, and she groaned with the intensity of the pleasure that rippled down her flesh like the wind skimming the bay.

Her soaked shirt clung to her skin, providing no barrier to Jim's hands as they glided downward to cup her breasts. His thumbs toyed with her nipples, making them stand out against the wet fabric. Each caress set off a new storm of physical sensation that shook her to her very core. Her body tingled with the heat of longing, and she arched closer to him.

His mouth moved slowly to one breast, closing over the shirt, and she gasped as molten pleasure spread through her. If she could command her shaking fingers, she'd rip the shirt away to feel his warm mouth on her bare flesh.

"I want to make love to you," he muttered hoarsely, "but I need to hear you say you want me."

Silence stretched between them like a strand of taut wire. *Tell him*, her starving body pleaded, but the words wouldn't come. The effort brought tears to her eyes.

She stared at him helplessly as he raised his head. A wry smile didn't quite reach his eyes. "I'm chipping away at your armor," he whispered, "slowly but surely. You'd better dig in your heels, Kate Flannery, because I'm going to have you yet." The tension in his jaw gave way gradually, and he frowned. "You're shivering. Come on. Get upstairs before you catch cold."

Kate watched him get his coat, suppressing a desire to fling her arms around him when he bent to brush his lips over her cheek. "Good night, Kate," he whispered.

"Good night." She leaned against the door when it closed behind him, her heart still pounding. Why did she keep fighting him? Her heart twisted with anguish, and her body throbbed with unfulfilled longing.

Fudge, dozing by the heat register, had no answer, and neither did she.

chapter

5

Buck had come home the night before Thanksgiving on temporary discharge from the nursing home — R and R, he called it — and now he hovered over Kate in the kitchen like an impresario just before curtain time. "Aren't you putting any whiskey in that stuffing?" he demanded as he hobbled around the kitchen on crutches.

"We're not drinking Thanksgiving dinner," Kate said firmly. "You can have wine with the meal."

"Hmmmph," he grunted, frowning as she scored the ham and stuck it with cloves. "Have we got any more of those brandied peaches in the cellar?"

Kate raised her eyebrows skyward and moaned, "Now don't go trying to get down those steps or you'll fall and break your other leg. And if the fall doesn't do it, I will. I'll get the peaches."

"A lot of trouble for some fella," Buck observed with a sparkle in his eye.

"He's alone this Thanksgiving," Kate said defensively.

"Mmm-hmmm. Did you get marshmallows for the sweet potatoes?"

"Yes, but I've never done them that way before. They might not turn out."

"Sure they will. Besides, this Jim'll be too busy looking at you to think about sweet potatoes."

"Buck," she said in exasperation, "Jim and I have only been working together a little over a week. One more word about him, and I'll . . . I'll ship you back to the nursing home before dinner." An inner demon laughed at her implication that she didn't consider Jim anything more than a co-worker, but she squelched it.

"You're cold-hearted, Katie," Buck teased her. "It's bad enough I have to check back in first thing in the morning."

"You know I'll miss you," she assured him in sudden seriousness. "But you'll be out soon. The doctor said your leg's healing."

"Well, I feel like a convict on parole, out for just one day."

"That's because in two days you'd be right back out on the skiff. What you really need is a body cast."

Buck chuckled in amusement, but he

stepped out of Kate's way while she finished stuffing the turkey. "I'm anxious to meet this Jim," he murmured, but Kate barely caught the amused undercurrent in his voice, and she let the remark pass.

Jim arrived promptly at three. Kate was bustling about the kitchen mashing the sweet potatoes for the casserole and trying to remember what she needed from the refrigerator. Buck answered the door and introduced himself as she turned off the electric mixer. "So you're the famous waterman I've heard so much about," Jim said with an engaging smile.

"Not so famous, just plenty old." Buck grinned back.

"Kate, I brought you a bottle of wine." She took it with a smile, and Jim added, "I wasn't sure what vintage went with snack cakes."

"No doubt Jeeves had that information at the ready," she retorted, and Buck threw them a quizzical glance.

"The imaginary butler Kate assumes caters to my every need," Jim explained. His eyes roved over Kate's red knit dress, and he gave a low, appreciative whistle.

Smiling, Kate popped the sweet potato casserole into the oven. "All right," she said. "we can eat in a few minutes." She got plates from the cupboard and turned to find Jim ready to take them from her. Buck sat down with satisfaction, laying his crutches on the floor, while Kate made gravy, then pulled the turkey from the oven. Jim was opening the wine, and Kate began carrying platters to the table — sliced ham, turkey with dressing, the sweet potato casserole, corn, hot rolls, gravy, and of course the cranberry sauce.

Jim held her chair for her, his fingers brushing her back as she sat down. She was discomfited to find Buck's bright eyes on her. He turned to Jim.

"I read in the paper that your aunt is having some kind of big dinner party today for a charity organization," he observed.

Kate had read that too, and her spirits had done a nosedive. All day she'd had visions of what Louise Andrews would serve for Thanksgiving — a capon or Cornish hens, something more exotic than roast turkey. If the potatoes were mashed, then they'd also be piped from a tube into delicate shapes. The vegetables would be smothered in rich sauces with French names. And for dessert Kate imagined a light, fluffy pumpkin mousse.

She glanced around the table in embarrassment. The gravy had lumps, the rolls were slightly burned, and the dressing tasted of too much sage. The food was so *ordinary*. She must seem like a country mouse to Jim.

"My aunt has lost sight of the meaning of Thanksgiving," Jim said dryly. "I've suffered through enough of her dinners to last a lifetime." He looked directly at Kate. "What I've missed are the meals my mother used to fix — just like this one."

Kate suddenly felt almost giddy with happiness.

Buck sighed. "Yeah, I bet she even had brandied peaches."

"I'll get your peaches," Kate said, rolling her eyes. "You're worse than a kid with candy." But she was grinning widely all the way down to the cellar.

It was obvious to Kate that Buck had taken to Jim right away. They talked about oystering and the bay and various watermen that Jim remembered from his boyhood. Buck even invited Jim to go goose hunting after he got his cast off.

After dinner Jim helped Kate clear away the dishes and insisted on washing. Buck remained at the table, resting his leg, smoking a small cigar, and continuing the conversation. "It'll be good to get back on the bay," he mused with a sigh. "Damn, but a room can feel like a prison cell when you can't do what you want."

Kate threw him a sympathetic glance. "It won't be long. You'll be back tonging with me soon enough."

"It can't be soon enough to suit me," Jim said sharply, and Kate looked at him in surprise. "I don't like to think of Kate out on that skiff alone."

"Me either," Buck muttered with knitted brows.

"I'll go out with her as long as I'm on vacation, but after that . . ." Jim's voice trailed off, and a pensive expression crossed his face. She knew what he was remembering, and she felt for him.

"I can start going out again as soon as that damn doctor lets me get back home," Buck said.

"You're both talking about me as if I were a child," Kate interjected tartly. "I can take care of myself. And as for you, Buck, you aren't getting near the skiff until the doctor gives his okay." She went back to vigorously drying dishes, her head lowered defensively.

She heard Jim's irritated snort, but ignored it. The tension was broken by a knock on the door. Buck called for whoever it was to come in.

A blast of chill air ushered in Red and Mike, who surveyed the scene with jovial expressions. "So you've got him doing dishes, do you, Katie?" Red called with a laugh. "I told you, Jim, that Kate's a rough captain. At least she's wearing the apron and not you."

"I wouldn't dream of crossing her," Jim bantered back, and the men broke into loud chuckles.

"So, Buck, you escaped for two nights anyway," Mike said with a wink. "What say we make the best of it? The boys are all waiting in the truck outside."

"Good lord!" Kate exclaimed. "He'll be a permanent fixture of that nursing home after you all get through partying."

"Now, Katie," Red cajoled her, "Buck needs some *therapy*. Why, I bet after tonight his leg'll feel as good as new."

"And his head'll be in a sling," Kate commented wryly. "Not to mention his backside after the doctor finds out."

"We'll get him to the home by morning," Red promised. A horn honked outside, and he added hastily, "Come on, Buck. Get your coat."

"I'll see you later, Katie," Buck said, a devilish grin on his face. "Nice to meet you, Jim. You two don't get into any fights while

117

I'm gone now. Maybe we ought to leave a referee."

Red and Mike broke into amused chortles, and Kate shot them a mock frown. "I'll be the soul of politeness," she promised in a sweet voice.

"Hah!" Mike laughed, and Kate pretended to get ready to throw the dishtowel at him. Laughing, the three men ducked out the kitchen door, Buck bringing up the rear on his crutches. "See you later, Katie," he called, and Kate smiled at the happiness in his voice. A night out with his friends would do him good.

"The last of the dishes." She sighed wearily as Jim poured the dirty water down the drain. "It seems futile, when you consider they'll only be dirty again in a few hours."

"How about another glass of wine?" Jim asked. "We could share a glass, so we wouldn't dirty two."

"Thanks, but I need a full serving to revive me." She sank down at the table, gratefully accepting the wine Jim offered, and watched as he took a seat opposite her.

"Dinner was delicious," he said. "Thanks for inviting me. I felt a real sense of family here. Not like at my aunt's."

"Thank you, but truthfully you must have

a cast-iron stomach or else you've spent considerable time in the diplomatic corps. I can hardly stand my own cooking myself. And Buck only refrained from complaining because you were here. Usually he soaks everything in catsup to drown the taste."

"Your cooking's fine."

She smiled back at him, then lapsed into silence, staring down into her wine. It had been one of her more pleasant Thanksgivings. It really hadn't mattered that the meal wasn't first-rate. They'd shared a kindred spirit . . .

"What are you thinking?" Jim asked suddenly, and Kate looked up guiltily. She'd been so lost in thought that she was almost surprised to see him across the table from her, watching her intently.

She took a deep breath and decided to be honest with him. "About Jeffrey," she said. Jim's face clouded momentarily, and she continued, "The last time he and I had Thanksgiving dinner together was two years ago. He grudgingly let me invite Buck — Jeffrey and I lived in an apartment in Easton then — and it was one of the worst meals I've ever eaten. Not the food, but the atmosphere. Buck didn't say a word, and Jeffrey just gulped down his food, then headed for the nearest tavern to watch the football game with his buddies."

"Game?" Jim inquired innocently, his raised eyebrows giving him away.

"The game!" Kate cried, jumping up. "You're missing the big football game. Come on."

"You really don't have to turn on the TV for me." Jim laughed. "I'm perfectly content sitting here talking to you."

"No, you aren't," Kate insisted, hurrying into the living room, Jim right behind her. "Now just sit down and make yourself comfortable."

Jim reclined against the couch, his hands laced behind his head, a satisfied smile on his face. Kate watched him from the corner of her eye. Her mouth went dry when she saw his arm muscles flex as he changed position, and she tried to force her attention to the game, which had just begun. But her thoughts were riveted on the man sitting so close to her, and her senses responded to his nearness. Her hands curled in her lap as she remembered his kiss, and once more she longed to tangle her fingers in his hair while his mouth possessed hers.

"Are you bored?" he asked, turning to her sympathetically.

"No, of course not," she assured him, feeling her face grow hot, as though he could read her thoughts.

"You sighed."

"Just a little tired, I guess," she hedged.

"Maybe if I explained the game to you, you might enjoy it more." She hid a smile as Jim continued. "The man with the football is the quarterback. He calls the plays. The center snapped it to him, and he's going for a pass. Watch him fade back and fake one before he finds his target. Look out!" Jim exclaimed suddenly. "Damn!" he added as the quarterback went down beneath a burly tackle. Jim groaned.

"Is that bad?" Kate asked with mock innocence.

Jim shot her a grimace. "Maybe you'd really rather do something else."

"No, no," she assured him. "I think I'm beginning to catch on. Let's see now. The quarterback who just got sacked is leading the league in ground yardage this season, but his throwing arm hasn't been worth a darn since he had that tendon problem. And the big fellow who tackled him is the new recruit from Ohio State who's been burning up the field in his first year. Back to the game — it's fourth down and nine yards to go. I'd say they'll punt." She glanced at Jim, trying not to smile. "How am I doing?"

He stared at her in amazement. "You're a

121

football fan?" he managed to choke out.

Kate nodded, letting her laughter spill over. "A confirmed Cowboys rooter. Their backfield is dynamite."

"To say the least," he murmured, still bemused. "I suppose I should have guessed. Growing up with no woman around, it's natural you would have taken on traditional male interests."

Now it was Kate's turn to arch her eyebrows. "Traditional male interests? Is that a roundabout way of saying I'm not feminine?"

"I meant it as a compliment," Jim said with a wry smile. "I must admit I've never known a woman with your versatility. And as for your femininity . . ." His voice faded, and Kate held his gaze as a different light came into his eyes. Her heart beat faster and sent heat coursing through her veins. Suddenly the room was like a hothouse, and she was the prize orchid.

She sat perfectly still, unable to move, as he reached out ever so slowly to touch her hair. He stroked it lightly, before his fingers curved down to her cheek. "No, Kate," he said in a husky voice, "there's no question about your femininity — or your desirability."

Her breathing quickened as his fingers

began to trace a delicate line over her full lips. She ached to feel his mouth on hers and leaned closer. He brushed a lock of hair from her cheek, then cupped her chin in both strong hands. She swallowed nervously as he bent slowly. When his mouth touched hers, she gave a gasp of pleasure, and his firm lips forced her mouth open, his tongue seeking entrance. Her eyes closed as though she were drugged, and she felt powerless in his hands, giving herself over to the pleasure he offered.

Her hands slid around his neck automatically, and she felt the coarse hair beneath her fingers. A warning was going off in her head again, telling her she was on the brink of losing herself. But she blocked it out as his kiss deepened.

His hand moved from her chin to her throat, following the pulsing cord there to the hollow and then it passed caressingly over her breast. Kate trembled — the sensations he was causing were burning all reason from her, all sanity. His every touch was turning her muscles and bones to explosive liquid. If a match had been struck, she was sure she would have burst into a consuming flame.

"You're beautiful, Kate," Jim whispered, his voice a seducing narcotic.

"Jim," she murmured against his lips, "please." She wanted more, much more, but coherent thought was impossible, and completing a sentence seemed beyond her capability.

Even as she strained closer to him, he drew back slowly, his eyes burning with emotion. His hands fell slowly away from her, and he leaned back. She parted her mouth on a ragged sigh, wanting him to continue, feeling his abandonment like a deep wound. She was starved for a caress, a touch, but instinctively she knew that it was only this man's touch that destroyed her defenses so completely.

All at once she realized that he'd misunderstood her ragged plea as a signal for him to stop, and she felt bereft, unable to convey her need.

The crowd on the TV screen was going wild, and slowly Jim's eyes swung to them. The instant replay filled the screen, and he gave a low whistle. "A forty-yard field goal. The second quarter and first time either of them made the scoreboard."

"A closer game than anyone expected," Kate breathed, her eyes still on Jim, feeling inane talking about football when she was aching with desire. He seemed to be putting what happened between them out of his mind, but she was still reeling from the effects. Her skin felt as though she had been caught in a rain of sparks.

"My aunt wants you to come to dinner at her house Sunday," Jim said casually, his eyes still on the TV. He locked his hands behind his head. "Are you free?"

"Yes," she said hesitantly. "What kind of dinner is it?"

"She wants to meet the infamous lady oyster tonger I've told her so much about. Dress is semi-formal."

"Semi-formal? What's that — high heels with my jeans?"

"How about a pants suit or a dress?"

"All right."

"By the way, this is for you." He pulled an envelope from his jacket pocket and held it out to her, his eyes still on the TV, though he was watching only a beer commercial. Curious, Kate took the envelope, which had her name typed on the front. The paper was quality bond, as was the stationery with the Carlisle Foundation letterhead. Kate scanned the letter, then reread it again quickly. Her grant had been reinstated! She was ecstatic. But immediately doubts assailed her.

"Are you responsible for this?" she asked in surprise.

"Does it matter?" He finally looked at her, and Kate saw embarrassment in his eyes. So he *was* responsible, and he didn't want her to know.

"It matters, Jim," she said quietly, frowning down at the letter in her lap. "I can't accept this on these terms. It wouldn't be fair to the others whose grants were canceled."

"Fair?" Jim said angrily. "Is it fair that you go out on a skiff by yourself in freezing weather and do the work of a man?"

"Is that why you did this? Because you don't think I'm capable of doing my work by myself?" Kate tilted her chin defiantly.

Jim shook his head in irritation, frowning. "Why do you insist on being so damn independent? Is that what your grandfather and his friends taught you when you were a little girl? Can't anyone take care of you just a little?"

"No!" she burst out bitterly. "I can take care of myself. I don't want anyone else trying to run my life."

"Caring for someone is not running their life," Jim retorted. He raked a hand through his hair and stood up, towering over her, his hands jammed into his jacket pockets. "One of these days, Kate Flannery, you're going to find out it's very lonely all by yourself, with nothing but independence to keep you warm."

Kate stood up angrily, ready to face him down, but something on the TV caught her eye. Jim's glance followed. The Carlisle Refinery logo was superimposed behind the newscaster, and both fell silent, listening to the story.

". . . stretching several miles down the Chesapeake." Film footage of the refinery came onto the screen, and the newscaster continued talking over it. "Coast Guard and EPA officials were unavailable for comment, but when contacted at the refinery, Martin Andrews, corporate head, dismissed reports that the spill was serious."

A big man in a business suit appeared on the screen, and when the sound came up, he was saying to the interviewer, "It was regrettable, but unpreventable. The community can rest assured that there is no danger to the wildlife at present." Andrews went on to say that clean-up procedures would begin within two days.

Another film came up on the screen, and the newscaster began talking about a jazz festival. The whole newscast lasted less than two minutes, then the football game came back on the screen.

Kate turned furiously to Jim. "You knew

about that spill before you came here today, didn't you?" she accused him. His jaw clenched, but he didn't answer her, and Kate laughed bitterly. "That's why you got my grant back, isn't it? It was just a pacifier. You dangled it in front of me so I'd overlook the Carlisle sins."

"The Carlisle sins, as you call them, aren't what you think," he snapped. "You judge before you have all the facts, Kate."

"I don't judge, Jim," she said coldly. "But the public will. And they won't let Carlisle Refineries get away with this."

"You don't even want to hear what I have to say about that spill, do you?" he demanded.

"No! Because you'd tell me some convenient little explanation to take all the blame off the refinery. You and your uncle are birds of a feather. You don't care about the bay. That was all lip service."

"Kate, listen to me." His voice was hard as he touched her arm, but she backed away.

"Don't touch me," she hissed. "Don't ever touch me again."

She saw something in his face alter, and it made her shiver even through the heat of her anger. "All right, Kate," he said in a voice of icy calm, "you've established your territorial boundaries. I won't touch you. That's a promise. But you want me, and you know it." He strode to the kitchen while Kate stood staring after him, paralyzed. He got his coat from the closet and shrugged into it, then turned at the door. She could see the deep anger in his eyes even from that distance. "You can't hide from me forever, Kate," he said in a low, menacing voice. "One day you'll admit what you're feeling. I'll make sure of that."

The door slammed behind him, and Kate sank onto the couch, trembling. How dare he threaten her! She'd never admit that she wanted him! Never! *Liar,* a little voice inside mocked her. *You would have said the words tonight, have said them all too easily. You do want him.*

She was still staring at the ceiling over her bed when Buck came stumbling into the house late that night, singing and bumping into the furniture. The singing went on until he was in his own bedroom, then the bed springs creaked, and the noise died down. Still Kate lay awake, Jim's harsh promise echoing in her ears.

chapter

6

Kate woke the next morning feeling vaguely uneasy. Her mouth was dry, and her eyes stung as if she'd been crying. Then she remembered her fight with Jim the night before and she sank back onto her pillow. She wanted to roll over and crawl back under the covers and forget about oysters for one day, but that was impossible. At least the hard work should take her mind off Jim.

She washed up wearily, then checked on Buck, who was still sound asleep. Kate didn't disturb him. She'd made arrangements for one of the neighbors to take him back to the nursing home later in the morning. There was no point in waking him now.

She made a pot of coffee, standing bleary-eyed at the kitchen window while the hot water dripped through the grounds. She clutched her terry cloth robe tightly around herself and stared out at the dark. Only a finger of dawn crept over the horizon, pale pink like a baby's cheek.

She remembered how Jim enjoyed the view from this window, and pressed her lips tightly together. He'd made his choice, and it had been Carlisle Refineries, not the bay. He had no right to enjoy what he was destroying.

She broke off her morose thoughts as the dripping of the water in the pot slowed to a stop. She poured herself a cup, then carried it to her bedroom to dress. When she was ready to leave, she slapped together a turkey sandwich and filled the thermos with coffee. It promised to be a long, cold, lonely day.

By the time she drove to the dock, more pale light was creeping over the bay, dusting the water with a ghostly haze. The skipjacks looked like sleeping giants, rocking at their moorings.

"Morning, Kate," Red called as he emerged from his pickup. "How's Buck doin' this morning? He need a cast for his head?"

Kate forced a smile and shook her head. "He was sound asleep, although I dare say he may feel a twinge of a headache when he wakes up."

"That he might." Red laughed. "The old boy put away a lot of beer last night. Said it was the first decent meal he'd had since he got thrown in that nursing home."

Mike, who had gotten out of the other side of the truck, ambled slowly around to Red's side. "Damned if we didn't have a good time last night though," he said, wincing as he ran his hand through his hair.

"Such a good time that you don't remember it?" Kate asked wryly.

"Things did get a mite fuzzy after the fourth pitcher," Mike admitted, and Red grinned.

"About as fuzzy as the inside of your eyeballs, I'd say," he added.

"Let's get to drudgin' then," Mike said. "The bay'll clear up my head real fast."

Kate waved to them and climbed aboard the *Kathryn D* to prepare for a long day of tonging. She knew the men would do a good day's work despite their headaches. Their lives were hard, and they liked to unwind in the evening. But none of them were drunks, and none ever abused another human being.

Lethargy hindered Kate's progress, and she took longer than usual getting ready to cast off, her feet dragging. The skipjacks were already nosing their pushboats into the water and shoving off from the dock while she was still setting out the tongs. Wearily she turned to start the engine, wondering where she should head today.

"Good morning," a crisp voice said from the dock. She spun around to see Jim standing there, a grim look on his face. There was a cool, dangerous air about him, which was emphasized by the dark shadow on his unshaven jaw. He was dressed in his usual work jeans, black windbreaker, and knit cap, the familiar canvas bag hanging from his hand.

"Go out with the dredgers if you're so fond of the bay," Kate said coldly, turning over the motor.

To her angry dismay, he hopped on board before she could cast off and threw the bag into the cabin. Turning to her, he said, "What are you afraid of? I'm only here to work."

"Don't you understand that I don't ever want you on my boat again?" she demanded, her voice rising. "And if you don't leave immediately, I'll get one of the dredgers to throw you off."

Jim glanced around with indolent ease. "I don't think so, Kate. They've all left."

She was so furious she could have cried with rage. All skipjacks were indeed too far away to hear her above the engine noise of the pushboats. "Damn you!" she cursed angrily. She cast off, pushing the throttle so that the skiff jerked away from the dock, but Jim seemed not the least perturbed. He stood watching her stonily for a moment, then disappeared inside the cabin.

Kate fumed all the way to Cove Point. He had no right to force himself on her like this. He could at least have had the decency to leave her alone. She wasn't even going to give him the satisfaction of acknowledging his presence. He could cull if he wanted, but she would pretend he wasn't there.

That plan was shortlived when she anchored, because he emerged from the cabin and picked up the tongs. Kate compressed her lips to bite back a protest — no matter what he did she wasn't going to speak to him. She put on the apron and took her position behind the work board.

They each poured angry energy into the work at hand. Jim slammed piles of oysters on the board in rapid succession. Kate's nimble fingers kept up with his furious pace, culling the keepers with an ease born of experience. The pile grew at a tremendous rate, Jim working as though fatigue were alien to him. Kate saw that he'd stripped down to his flannel shirt, which was plastered to his back with sweat. For a moment she worried that he would catch cold, then she shoved her concern to the back of her mind. He was responsible for himself — his health wasn't any of her business.

He stood massaging his arms while she culled the latest batch, then he eyed the pile of keepers. "Lunchtime," he announced in a flat tone.

She didn't look at him or acknowledge that he'd spoken, but after a minute of silence he headed for the cabin, and Kate stood up and stretched. Out of the corner of her eye she saw him sit down at the small table, and she shivered. She needed to warm up, but she wasn't about to get herself alone in that cramped cabin with Jim Carlisle.

Damn! It was her cabin, not his. She strode inside and hurriedly poured herself some coffee from her thermos, conscious of him sitting at the table, his eyes practically burning a hole in her back. She could smell pungent mustard — a glance at his lunch had revealed a ham sandwich and warm baked beans. Her stomach churned in hunger, but she turned to leave anyway. Her turkey sandwich was in the refrigerator, and she'd have to step close to him to get it.

She stopped short when he leaned casually against the door jamb, completely blocking her path, and offered her a sardonic smile. "Sit down and eat your lunch. I assume you brought one."

Kate glowered at him, discomfited by the cool insolence in his eyes. Abruptly she spun around, jerked open the refrigerator door and pulled out her sandwich. "Satisfied, Mr. Carlisle?" she inquired with mock sweetness as she held it up.

His eyebrows rose. "So we're back to formality."

"We aren't even back to speaking," she hissed.

"But it seems we are," he retorted. "Now sit down and listen."

"I have no intention of listening to anything you have to say."

"Sit down." Something in his voice and eyes warned her that the wisest course would be to do as he ordered.

"Do you always treat women in such a high-handed, chauvinistic manner?" she demanded, sitting at the table nevertheless, choosing the side farthest from him.

"Only when they're so incredibly stubborn and self-righteous that nothing short of a club will get their attention. Has it occurred to you that your attitude toward the business world is also chauvinistic?"

Kate glared at him impotently, noting that he still blocked the door as if convinced that she would bolt the cabin and throw herself into the bay if forced to listen to him. "Speak your piece and let's get it over with," she snapped.

He crossed his arms over his chest, and she thought how much he looked like a modern-day pirate with his rumpled hair falling onto his forehead and the lean lines of his face emphasized by his cold anger. His eyes still burned, and she shuddered, remembering how they'd burned with a different emotion the night before. Even now her heart beat faster when she thought of it. Damn her senses for betraying her anyway! Why couldn't she just hate him without ambivalence, without her heart pounding and her mouth going dry every time he was near her.

"Carlisle Refineries will take full blame for the spill and shoulder the cost of cleanup." He watched her carefully from under heavy lids, his face still hard with anger.

Her derisive snort was his answer, and Jim's jaw tightened. "I talked to my uncle last night," he said, "and convinced him that the best course of action would be to wash our dirty linen publicly."

The wry emphasis on the word "convinced" didn't elude Kate, and she regarded him suspiciously. "What do you mean? How big a part did you have in his decision?"

Jim sighed, and Kate noticed suddenly how tired he looked, as though he'd been up all night before throwing himself into the oyster tonging today.

"All right, Kate, the truth. The spill was from a pump I told Martin to replace two years ago. It leaked into the bay from the check valve in a pipe that I'd also warned him about. I've been trying for a year now to get him to try some of my ideas for pollution control, but he wouldn't agree. Last night I talked to him for hours and finally threatened to go public with my own complaints if he didn't shoulder the responsibility for the spill. That's it, Kate — my cards are all on the table."

Her angry resolve began to waver in the face of his explanation, and she tried to bolster it. "What about the grant?" she asked in a firm voice. "Wasn't that an attempt to mollify me before I found out about the spill?"

Jim shook his head. "I arranged for the grant days ago. I'll admit I knew about the spill last night — my uncle called me when it happened, and we argued — but I didn't want it to ruin Thanksgiving for you."

"You were so angry," she accused him. She knew she was being unfair, but her feathers were still ruffled by their angry parting.

138

Jim laughed shortly and without humor. "Angry hardly covers the range of my emotions last night, my dear. I tried to do something for you because I don't want you out on this bay by yourself anymore, and you turned on me like a spitting wildcat." Apparently assured that she wasn't about to jump up and run away, he moved slowly and wearily to the table and sat down opposite her. He rested his forehead on his hands, then looked at her somberly.

Kate took a deep breath and laced her fingers tightly. "Why don't you want me on the water alone, Jim? Is it because of your father?"

He hesitated before answering, conflicting emotions flickering in his eyes. For a brief moment Kate thought she saw a deep tenderness there, and in that instant her breath was suspended, but he shut his eyes against her probing gaze. "Things happen, Kate," he said in a low, pained voice. "Things we can't foresee or prevent. I can't always be here to protect you." He caught her glance and smiled dryly. "And don't accuse me of being a chauvinist because I feel like protecting you."

"Are you a chauvinist?" she asked softly, smiling at him tentatively.

"It would be rather impossible around

you, wouldn't it?" he answered grimly. "No, I'm not, if you're talking about equality in life and marriage. But I do have strong feelings about one person's responsibility to another, not financial but emotional. Maybe that sounds chauvinistic to you, but I believe in fidelity and trust."

"That sounds like a bank — First Fidelity and Trust," she joked, and the lines of tension around his eyes relaxed.

"And you, Kate, are you a liberated woman who considers those ideas antiquated?"

She shook her head, suddenly serious. "It's all I'd ask of someone. That and love."

His eyes met hers in a searching gaze, and she looked away first, disconcerted. Love and fidelity and trust were all too believable when she looked into Jim's face. But she'd never found them before, and she'd been hurt trying. He seemed to read her thoughts, and asked softly, "You can't make yourself believe or trust yet, can you, Kate?"

She shook her head and gave a nervous laugh. "You're beginning to know me too well."

"And knowing you well," he sighed, "I'm guessing that you still won't accept the grant."

"I can't. I'm sorry."

"All right. I'll let it go for now." He rested his head on his hands again, rubbing his eyes, and Kate realized that he must be exhausted.

"We've got enough oysters for the day," she said. "Why don't you lie down and rest. I'll start the skiff back to the dock."

"On one condition — you have a decent lunch first. Here, I brought a ham sandwich for you and some extra potato salad and beans."

She acquiesced, hunger eroding her independence. Besides, food was one way he took care of her that she'd grown accustomed to, actually looked forward to. Don't get mellow, old girl, she told herself. You haven't turned into a clinging vine yet.

She dug into her lunch, and Jim curled up on the small bed in the cabin. In a few minutes he was asleep, his breathing deep and easy, and Kate found herself studying him almost without thinking about it. He was facing her, and curled up asleep he looked particularly vulnerable. The lines on his face had softened, his mouth relaxed into a gentle curve. But if he was charming in sleep, Kate was all too aware that he was even more so awake. Despite his temper, she reminded herself. *His temper?* her conscience nagged. *What about your own?*

She finished eating and stood up quietly to weigh anchor and start back when he murmured and turned restlessly in his sleep. She stopped at the door, hesitating to infringe on his privacy, but wondering if he was all right. One hand was flung over the side of the bed, and he clenched it tightly in his sleep. He murmured again, and Kate caught what sounded like a name. She frowned and went back onto the deck, her eyes clouded in concentration. Automatically she set about preparing to start back, her mind on Jim.

The name he'd murmured in his sleep had sounded like Leora. Kate ground her teeth together as she started the engine and swung the skiff around. It shouldn't matter to her if he was dreaming about his dead wife — but it did matter. For some reason it bothered her a great deal that he carried her memory so secretly. He had never talked to Kate about Leora, and he seemed loath to bring up the subject. Why then did she invade his dreams? Was he still married to a ghost?

Jim was still sleeping when she docked at the buyer's wharf. Kate shook him gently awake after the oysters had been weighed, and she'd been paid. She was still disturbed about what she'd heard, and she hesitated before touching his shoulder. Even asleep he was compelling. Warmth spread through her hand as she touched him, and as soon as he began to wake up groggily she drew back.

"Are we there already?"

She nodded. "Here's your pay for today."

He stuffed the money into his shirt pocket with a wry look at her. Slowly he sat up and ran his hand through his hair. "I don't need the money, you know."

"I know, but I feel better paying you. End of discussion."

"Aye, aye, Captain," he muttered with feigned meekness.

When they were walking to their cars, he turned as if a thought had just struck him. "You're still coming to dinner Sunday, aren't you?"

She had forgotten about that, and now she tried to mask her confusion. "I . . . I don't know. I hadn't thought about it."

"Please come. My aunt is expecting you."

"All right. I'll polish my sneakers." She hesitated, then asked, "Will your uncle be there?"

Jim shrugged, his eyes narrowing. "I don't know. Generally he doesn't bother with my aunt's social luncheons. Goes to the club to play racquetball or something."

"You sound rather disapproving."

"Let's just say that my Uncle Martin is a far cry from my dad. To Dad, family was everything, and the business or even oystering came second. I figure he had his priorities straight." He held her car door open for her, then looked down as she slid behind the wheel. "See you Sunday, Kate."

By early Sunday afternoon Kate had changed clothes at least five times. Finally she settled on a wool skirt and silky print blouse, both in earth tones. She'd washed her hair, and despairing of doing anything fancy given its straight nature, she'd merely blown it dry and stuck a fancy clip in the side. She usually wore little makeup, but today she dusted on a light blue eye shadow and used mascara on her lashes. A touch of pink lipstick, a pair of gold earrings, and she was ready.

When Jim knocked on the door she was feeding Fudge. She called for him to come on in. He surveyed her for a minute, then broke out laughing. She looked up in surprise.

"You make such a contrast," he said. "You look gorgeous, and there you are dishing up dog food." His laughter died down, though a sparkle remained in his eyes. "You're a dichotomy, Kate. Do you know that? A lovely riddle. Every time I see you it's like a breath of fresh air."

"What flattery." She smiled, washing her hands. "You'll turn my head."

"I doubt that," he replied. "You're also totally impervious to my attempts to charm you. Shall we go brave my aunt?"

She wasn't exactly impervious to his charms, Kate thought wryly as she got her coat. Seeing him today in a charcoal blazer and black slacks with a black turtleneck sweater, she felt a flush of longing.

Louise Carlisle Andrews's home was on the Eastern Shore near St. Michaels. The house was situated right on the bay. House? Kate thought wryly. Mansion was more accurate.

Jim must have noticed her glassy-eyed look as he turned the Porsche into the winding black-topped driveway because he said, "This house was built in the early eighteenth century, and my aunt and uncle have renovated it. They've at least tried to preserve its character, something I give them credit for."

"It's beautiful," Kate breathed. The enormous white frame home stood at the end of the drive. The grounds were neatly manicured with large stands of trees on either side, many of them quite old, judging from the massive girth of their trunks.

A young blond maid whom Jim introduced as Paula opened the door.

Jim led Kate past a winding wooden staircase through a spacious, rich-hued hallway with striped wallpaper and several walnut curio pieces toward the back of the house. On either side of the hall double doors opened onto various rooms, each furnished in the style of the 1700s. There was a fireplace in each room, no two exactly alike, from the mantel to the tile. Primitive paintings and prints of wildlife hung on the walls.

They entered a warm, airy room with a terrace overlooking the bay. At the far end of the room Jim's aunt sat playing a grand piano. Kate recognized the piece as one of Schubert's.

She was a thin woman in her sixties, her gray hair arranged in a curly style that just reached her ears. Her face was strong, yet held a certain vulnerability as the bright brown eyes followed the music score in front of her.

She finished with a flourish and sat back with her eyes closed. In the ensuing silence Jim and Kate began to clap. Louise Andrews opened her eyes in apparent surprise, then smiled at them. "I'm sorry. I didn't hear you two come in." She rose and greeted them with a gracious smile, taking Kate's hand at Jim's introduction and saying how pleased she was to meet her. But Kate detected a slight coolness in her tone that made her uneasy.

"Your view of the bay is magnificent," she said.

For a moment Louise Andrews's eyes darkened, and her voice was low when she replied, "I really would have preferred my piano in a different room, but the light was best here."

Just then Paula announced lunch, and they followed Louise to the dining room.

It was another large room with a cherry table and six high-backed chairs. A bowl of carnations and snapdragons graced the center, and Kate glanced around at the rest of the room as Jim seated her in the chair Louise indicated. Directly across from her was a cherry buffet, and Kate's breath caught when she saw a photograph in a silver frame. It was Jim and Leora — Kate recognized her from the wedding photograph in the newspaper. They were standing on the deck of what looked like a cabin cruiser, and Jim was smiling, his arm around Leora's waist. She was laughing, her head tilted slightly so that her hair brushed Jim's shoulder.

Kate couldn't stop staring at the picture. She tore her eyes away only after Jim had seated his aunt and moved to take his own chair across from Kate. She could still see the picture just to the right of him. It was like looking into a double mirror. There was Jim in front of her, giving her a conspiratorial smile that she knew was intended to dispel her nervousness, while to the right was a smaller version of Jim smiling with another woman.

"Jim tells me you tong for oysters," Louise said, her eyes swinging to Kate.

"Temporarily," she said. "I'm a marine biologist, but my research grant —" She broke off and flushed guiltily, then continued in a quieter voice, "I'm not doing research right now, so I go tonging."

"That's a demanding job for a woman." Louise passed the bowls and platters that Paula was setting on the table. There was poached salmon, green beans vinaigrette, corn pudding, and a potato casserole with bits of sausage in it.

Kate accepted the salmon with a polite thank you and said, "It is pretty tiring, but my grandfather will get the cast off his leg soon, and then he'll be going out with me."

"You go out on the water by yourself?"

Louise asked, her voice sharp.

"Not lately. Jim's been working with me — I give him all the credit for the fact that I haven't had to use the heating pad on my arms since he first started tonging with me." She smiled at Louise, but her smile died when the other woman grew suddenly pale.

"You've been out on the bay?" she demanded, turning to Jim, her voice and face filled with terror. Kate stared at her, unnerved by the depth of her reaction.

"Just the couple of weeks I'm off," he said in a soothing voice, calmly dishing out green beans.

"How could you after what happened?" she continued in a low voice filled with horror. Jim clenched his jaw and looked at her, but he said nothing, and Louise turned to Kate accusingly. "His father — my brother — was drowned on the bay. Surely you knew that."

"Jim told me," Kate said quietly, groping for something to say that would calm the woman. "I'm terribly sorry. It must have been a great loss."

"Loss?" Louise snorted in disbelief. "Peter was my younger brother. I nearly raised him myself. Loss? No, it was more than that. It was nearly the end of the world. But Jim was left. I helped put him through school because Peter had chosen to be a waterman and he had no money of his own. Our father cut him off when he wouldn't go into the business." Her eyes were clouded with grief, and her voice choked as she continued the story. "Father would never let me see or talk to him. It was only after Father died that I was able to go to Peter and see Jim for the first time. Then the bay took my brother."

Suddenly Kate understood why Louise Andrews didn't like having her piano in the room overlooking the Chesapeake.

Jim sighed heavily and shook his head. "There's no point in even talking about this. All we're doing is causing bad feelings and making Kate uncomfortable."

Lunch continued under an oppressive silence, broken only by Jim's light attempts at conversation.

"Jim, you must go visit some of your old friends soon," his aunt finally said, recovering her composure. "They've all been asking about you. Just the other day I saw Denise Sherill's mother in the store. She said poor Denise misses you terribly."

"*Poor* Denise is so busy being the biggest socialite on the Eastern Shore that she probably doesn't even think about me," Jim said sarcastically. "Her picture's always in the paper for one activity or another. What did she do to her husband anyway — party him to death?"

"Jim and Denise used to be quite an item," Louise explained patiently to Kate, sending Jim a disapproving glance.

"An item?" he repeated incredulously. "I took her out exactly twice, at your request, and I nearly died of boredom each time. Her vocabulary consists solely of the words Neiman-Marcus and Halston. Nothing comes between her and her Calvin Kleins, including her brain."

Kate smothered a smile, and Louise sighed in exasperation. "All right Jim, but you really should get out and mix some."

"I'm mixing just fine," Jim said gently, his eyes on Kate.

Frowning, Louise rang the bell for Paula and notified her briskly that they would have brandy in the living room.

As they stood up to leave, Louise added, "Granted, Denise is no Leora, but she has her qualities. And Mariette is still single, you know." Louise glanced at Kate and gave a cool explanation. "Mariette is Leora's younger sister."

Jim's noncommittal grunt gave no indication of his feelings, and Kate looked self-consciously back over her shoulder at the photo on the buffet. She tried to dismiss the uneasiness that washed over her — it was the way she'd felt as a child when she waded out into water that threatened to get deep suddenly — but the feeling persisted through the rest of the afternoon.

When it was time to leave, Jim went to Paula to get their coats, and Kate was left alone with Louise in the living room. Sunset had come early as usual at that time of the year, and though there was a crackling fire in the fireplace, it gave off little warmth to the room. Kate had felt a stiff formality between her and Jim's aunt since the moment they'd met, and their time together had done nothing to dispel it.

"Thank you for inviting me," Kate said quietly. "I had a lovely afternoon."

The eyes that met hers weren't unkind, but there was no warmth in them either. "I'm sorry about my outburst over the bay and watermen," Louise apologized softly, "but it's a subject that disturbs me deeply."

"That's all right," Kate assured her. "It must have been very painful."

The smile on Louise's lips was coolly polite, and Kate stiffened unconsciously. "I do want to thank you for providing Jim with a pleasant diversion during his vacation. I'm sure you've helped him keep his mind off Leora for a while at least. I don't think he'll ever be over her completely, but it helps if he keeps busy. It was nice meeting you, dear."

Kate murmured her good-byes as Jim returned with her coat. Once in the car, she fell silent, brooding over what Louise had said. From all indications, Jim and Leora had been quite close, and her death had had a devastating effect on him. Louise had implied that Jim was still grieving.

"I'm sorry she upset you," he said quietly.

Kate was startled. She glanced at him in the near darkness of the car, then said carefully, "It's all right. She feels betrayed by the bay. She's had a cruel loss."

Jim's eyes met hers briefly before he looked back at the road. "And?" he asked softly.

Kate flushed. Sometimes it seemed as if he read her thoughts, or else he was so attuned to the nuances of her speech that he detected every little hesitation. "And I think she's terrified of losing you."

He nodded. "I've tried to maintain a certain distance between my aunt and myself without rejecting her. It's not good for her to be so dependent on me. After all, it's

Martin she should lean on."

"But your uncle isn't there most of the time," Kate commented.

"Right." Jim sighed. "We all have to learn to deal with our private losses in our own way." He turned to Kate with renewed interest. "Something else is bothering you though. What is it?"

"Nothing." She shook her head quickly.

He gave her a penetrating stare, but when she remained silent he turned back to the road with a frown. Kate gave an inward sigh of relief that he hadn't pursued an answer and turned her thoughts away from Louise and Leora.

Jim saw her to the door but said he wouldn't come in. "I have to be at work early tomorrow," he said softly. "I have a lot of things to discuss with Martin." There was a hardness to his tone that puzzled her, but he didn't elaborate.

"Well, good night," Kate said uncertainly.

"Good night," he murmured, a mesmerizing light in his eyes as he stared down at her. Kate held her breath, feeling the familiar pounding of her heart as she stared back at him. She leaned slightly forward in longing, wanting suddenly to feel those hard arms around her and sensual lips teasing her own into response. His hand cupped her jaw, his thumb caressing her chin. He kissed the base of her throat first, and Kate sighed in exquisite pleasure. Her desire leaped to flames with each touch of his gentle hand on her lips and throat. He pushed aside the front of her wrap-around coat, his hand closing over her breast, fingers teasing and exciting. Kate moaned, and his lips touched hers lightly. She strained closer, but he wouldn't deepen the kiss, though she craved more.

He lifted his head slowly. "I guess I'll head on home," he drawled, one side of his mouth turning up in a lazy, mocking smile. He rested an arm on the door frame and looked down at Kate in amusement.

Her blood came to a simmer as she realized what he was doing — teasing her until she admitted she wanted him. She swallowed hard, determined not to give in to him, and he levered himself away from the door. "Good night, Kate."

Anger paralyzed her. He was already at his car before her legs would move. She stormed into the kitchen, slamming the door and throwing her coat onto a chair. Although she'd never been much of a drinker, tonight she threw restraint to the wind and poured herself a glass of whiskey from Buck's jug. But even after she'd emptied the

glass with a final grimace, Jim's words rang
in her ears — *One day you'll admit you want
me as much as I want you.*

chapter

7

Jim met Kate at the boat early Tuesday morning. She felt a pall still hanging over them, but whether it was her own uncertainty concerning Jim or the emotional distance he seemed to be deliberately putting between them, she wasn't sure. To further compound her testy mood, the engine wouldn't start.

She was cursing it while Jim worked futilely when Red called from his skipjack, "If you two can't get that old garbage scow to run, I could use a coupla extra hands, by golly."

"Are you sure?" Kate asked uncertainly.

"You bet. Flu got two more of my men yesterday. Come on aboard."

George McGruder's engine repair business was near the dock, so Kate ran over there quickly. "George'll fix it up for you," Red assured her when she joined them on board.

"I hope so," she said, frowning. "Buck'll raise hell if anything happens to that skiff."

The crew lowered the pushboat into the water, and with its nose against the stern of the skipjack, they began easing away from the dock. There was a flurry of activity on other skipjacks moored at the dock, and one by one other pushboats were lowered into the water. Once they were out on the Chesapeake, the pushboat motor was cut and it was hauled back aboard. Working together as a team, the crew raised the sails. As the wind caught them, the *Bountiful Harvest* swept along the bay.

"Ain't it a pretty sight?" Red called over the wind to Kate and Jim. They nodded in admiration as a flock of geese circled over the sails, then swooped down to land on a marsh. "Smartweed and millet's plentiful this year," Red commented. "More geese'n I've seen in ages."

"Everyone'll have wild goose for Christmas for sure," Kate commented.

"Oysterin's been good, too," Mike called out in agreement. "Be a good Christmas all the way around."

"Especially if you get your boy that there motorcycle, eh?" Red teased him.

"Reckon so." Mike grinned back.

There was a large oyster ground between Poplar Island and Tilghman Island, and Red turned the skipjack toward it. Kate reveled in the chill air that flapped the sails and blew her hair back from her face. She looked over at Jim and saw the same exhilaration mirrored on his face. For a brief moment they seemed to have experienced something beautiful and never-changing.

The crew headed to the cabin for morning coffee, and Kate and Jim followed, smiling at each other. All eight crew members slumped around the small table in the cabin. Mugs of coffee in hand, they munched donuts and quietly told stories and ribbed each other until they heard a shout from Red. Then everyone drained their mugs and hurried out on deck. Jim touched Kate's arm as they moved with the others, and a shock ran through her, so electrifying that she nearly groaned out loud. When she dared a glance at him, she saw that his jaw was tight and his eyes narrowed, and she wondered if it was the result of the fleeting contact or merely a reaction to the work ahead.

Barking instructions from his position at the wheel, Red ordered the crew to reef the mainsail as he drew near the spot he wanted to work. When they were ready, he gave another shout and men leaped to throw the dredges overboard. When they were played out over the oyster bar, Red increased the speed of the small engine that would reel the dredges back on board. Mike engaged the clutch, and the oyster-laden dredges began the laborious trip to the surface. The crew raced to grab the netting connected to each dredge and dump the catch it contained.

It was tough work, and Kate was warm in no time. Like the others, she soon peeled off her jacket, then went back to feeding the heavy dredges over the boat. Looking like iron box kites, the row of dredges disappeared into the water. Red maneuvered the big sailboat back and forth over the oyster bar, gathering oysters, then reeling in the dredges.

Kate grew tired, but she pressed on, determined to do her share of the work. She was strong, but lately she'd mostly culled while Jim had tonged, and her muscles had grown used to the easier labor.

They'd been working most of the morning, and her legs and arms were tired. A series of swells from a passing ship rocked the boat, and Kate suddenly lost her footing on the rolling deck.

She fell against Jim, who was working by her side, and instantly his hands closed on her arms to hold her steady. Immediately the rocking sensation moved inside her, and her balance seemed to have permanently deserted her. Jim's hands tightened, and Kate's heart thumped madly. The muscled strength holding her was doing strange things to her senses, and she murmured incoherently, her fingers stealing up to his chest.

"Do you have something you want to tell me?" Jim taunted mockingly, and Kate suddenly realized that she'd literally played into his hands.

"I have nothing to say to you," she snapped, stiffening in his embrace. "Now let me go."

Jim's voice dripped with honey-coated concern. "But you don't have your balance back, sweetheart. I wouldn't want you to fall." One hand began playing insolently with the hair at the nape of her neck, and Kate choked back a groan.

"My balance is fine," she hissed. "Now let go of me."

"None of that on board!" Red hollered good-naturedly, and the crew broke out in a chorus of laughter.

"So this is what you two do all day! And here you told everyone you was tongin'."

Kate gritted her teeth and jerked her arm away from Jim. "Watch your footing, sweetheart," he called after her with feigned solicitude as she marched away.

Jim worked beside her for the rest of the morning, leaning close each time he dumped a dredge, his hand deliberately brushing hers. Kate made an effort to control her wayward pulse, but after an hour of his teasing, her heart raced every time he stepped close to her. He always took pains to prolong the contact just until desire overrode her anger, then he'd move away again.

Kate's nerves were strung as tightly as the chain pulling in the dredges when she turned from dumping a load and plowed into Jim's chest. "Would you please move," she muttered through clenched teeth, her eyes on his shirt buttons.

"My, but we're crabby today," he said sweetly. "Did we get up on the wrong side of the bed?"

"We did not sleep in the same bed," Kate snapped, raising her head to glare at him.

He grinned down at her insolently. "I could remedy that."

"You . . . you!" she sputtered, at a loss of words. Sudden visions of her and Jim in bed together were swamping her control.

The other crew members were beginning to look at them, and Jim immediately assumed a conversational tone. "You have mud all over your face, sweetheart," he murmured, reaching up to run his fingers over her cheeks. Anger only served to heighten her senses. At his touch her blood ran in a molten torrent. He trailed his thumb across her lips, and her mouth parted helplessly, unable to put up even token resistance. "That's better, honey," he said with a devilish grin, and he turned and walked away.

Fury, desire, and overwhelming frustration ignited in Kate like a powder keg and, swooping down, she snatched up an oyster shell and hurled it at Jim. Her hands were shaking, and the shell missed, falling harmlessly on deck. Jim turned toward her, his expression amused, but she swallowed when she saw his flinty eyes. The determination in them promised only one conclusion to this game of his.

Kate spun around and went back to work, her back arched like an angry kitten's.

The crew broke for lunch late that morning. There was a cooler of beer to go with bologna sandwiches. Kate and Jim were sitting on the floor of the cabin, their backs against the wall. Jim lazily stretched his leg out full length against hers. Kate's muscles stiffened automatically, though she tried to hide it. But he further aggravated her by stretching his arms over his head, letting his shoulder brush hers as he did so.

She threw him a black look, but he only smiled innocently at her, amusement glinting in his eyes.

Irritated, Kate moved farther away from him, but he followed, and she again found herself in close contact with that muscular leg. Giving up, she sat rigidly, hardly tasting her lunch, every nerve tingling each time he brushed his leg against hers. Her temper was rising as fast as her temperature, and when lunch was over she leaped up and rushed back out on deck. "Whoa!" Red called. "I never seen a drudger so eager to get back to work."

"Maybe she's bored just sittin' around with the fellas," another crew member chortled.

"When they're young and pretty like that, they get more than enough male company all the time," Mike called, and the men burst out laughing.

"To an old drudger even a barnacle looks young and pretty," she shot back, and their laughter increased.

"She got you that time, Mike," Red called.

Slowly the men returned to work. Jim took his place beside Kate, making sure his arm touched hers several times while they hauled the dredges. They'd made their limit by late afternoon, and with the sails billowing in the wind, they started back for the buyer's wharf. Kate retreated to the cabin once they were underway and sat at the table drinking coffee with the rest of the tired crew. She was rubbing her lower back when Jim walked past her on his way to the coffee pot. With a solicitous, "Does your back hurt?" he began deftly massaging her.

Goaded into anger, she straightened up immediately and snapped, "It's just fine, thank you."

Jim sauntered on to the stove, casting a wickedly amused smile at her over the heads of the men. Kate glared back at him, noting with dismay that the dredgers were exchanging knowing winks, as though she and Jim had had a lovers' spat.

The trip back seemed to take forever. Once docked, and with the oysters weighed, Kate took the money Red paid her, thanked him, and left as fast as she could.

Jim was still waiting in line with the rest of the crew, and Kate breathed a sigh of relief as she rounded a corner out of his sight. The first order of business was to check on her skiff's engine. She found George McGruder in his shop. "It should be okay now, Katie," he assured her. "It's an old one, though. Goin' to conk out on you again soon, I bet.

Tell Buck he ought to get a new one."

"All right. Thanks, George." She paid him and headed for her car. At least she would be back on her own boat the next morning.

But as she neared the car, the tall figure leaning against it looked all too familiar, and her temper rose. "What kind of game have you been playing?" she demanded hotly when she drew near. "What were you doing today?"

"Did it bother you, Kate?" he asked softly.

"I . . . no . . . I don't care what you do," she stammered.

"Don't you really?" he demanded in a quiet voice, straightening up. One arm snaked out and curved around her back, pulling her abruptly against his hard length. She was breathless, and her fingers pressed against his chest, at first in protest and then in a caress. She lifted her head to his, waiting, but he only stared down at her, his eyes implacable. "No, Kate," he said softly. "I meant what I said. Being near you bothers me like hell, but with us, it's got to be a two-way street. All or nothing."

Angry, she pushed herself away from him, and turned her back to hide her trembling. "Damn you," she said softly.

"I know I'm making this hard on you," he said more gently, "but I want you to be sure you know what you want."

"And you're the best judge of what I want?" she demanded in a hoarse whisper.

"I'm sorry." He sighed. "I've wanted you so much that my patience is gone. I know you want me." When she flinched, he put a hand on her shoulder and added, "There's nothing wrong with that, Kate. But I won't repeat what happened today. I was pushing. I just thought I could make you realize that you're human after all."

Kate turned around slowly, and his hand fell from her shoulder. "Not human?" she said. "Is that how you see me?"

"No," he said softly, "that's how you see yourself. You won't allow yourself any emotions except safe ones — oh, maybe a little anger here and there, but nothing too serious. Nothing that might get you hurt."

Kate swallowed hard and stared back at him. She didn't know what to say — she was overwhelmed by his assessment of her. As always, he seemed to see through her defenses and read things that she had thought no one else knew.

He smiled at her and touched her nose lightly. "You don't always have to be strong, Kate. Don't you know that?"

"No," she said honestly. "I've always had to be."

"I guess you have," he admitted slowly. "That's tough for anyone." He drew a deep breath and surveyed her with a different expression, then broke out of his reverie. "See you tomorrow then, Kate."

"All right," she said, distracted. "Tomorrow." She watched him get into his car and wave to her before he drove off. Then she stood leaning against her own car. *What was he doing to her?*

But even as she asked, she knew the answer. Her skin was still warm and tingling where he'd touched her, and just the memory stirred her blood. Being with him was like living on the edge of the world where sky and water met, where storms were born.

What was he doing to her, she demanded again. "He's making me fall in love with him," she murmured softly, and the realization rocked her with a jolt that went right off the Richter scale.

Only a gray haze greeted Kate the next morning when she woke up. She hurried to the dock, shivering. It was the kind of day that heralded the first snowfall of winter, and usually she would have stayed home, but today she needed the physical labor to work out her tension.

The skipjacks stood like shadowy sentinels at the dock, their bare masts tall and ghostly in the gray dawn. The hum of the Porsche's motor came out of the haze as Kate got out of her car, and she waited for Jim to park. "Looks like winter's really here," he observed, glancing at the sky.

"Not many skipjacks going out today," she said, looking up and down the dock. One or two were being outfitted for the day, but most of the men had probably congregated at the general store to drink coffee and play cards.

When they were ready to go, the engine started right up, and Kate nodded in satisfaction. She set their course toward the Choptank River, and Jim brought her a cup of coffee. She leaned back and cast a critical eye on the clouds hovering on the horizon.

There would certainly be snow by evening at least.

Jim was standing near her, and she tensed, almost expecting him to touch her, but he didn't. Apparently the game was over. He'd told her why he'd done it, and now the next move was up to her.

She could no longer deny that he was right. She wanted to make love to him —

God, how she wanted to! And there was a growing bond between them. But she couldn't do it lightly, and with Jim she demanded a commitment equal to her own.

She turned back to the skiff, staring out at the Chesapeake as she adjusted their course. Something was wrong, but she couldn't say exactly what. Maybe it was only her imagination, but the skiff's engine seemed to hum at a different pitch today. Still, that was natural since George had worked on it.

After they'd anchored at the Choptank River, they began work without speaking. Somehow the silence was harder on Kate than the noisy bantering of the skipjack crew the day before. The fact that Jim was making a point of not getting near her only increased her tension. There seemed to be a magnetic force drawing them irresistibly together, and Kate believed that only sheer force of will kept her from stumbling into his arms. Jim was clearly waging a war as difficult as her own, and she caught him casting hungry glances at her all morning.

The tension between them mounted as the day wore on, and the increasing cloudiness seemed oppressive. She gritted her teeth whenever he dumped a new load of oysters on the work board. Her mind wasn't on culling, and she couldn't keep up with Jim. He dumped another pile on the board, and she glanced up at him in irritation, snapping, "Give me a break, for heaven's sake."

He leaned on the tongs, regarding her for a moment, then with narrowed eyes he turned and went back to work, his shoulders tense.

By late morning she was hungry, but the silence between them remained unbroken. Jim continued to work at a furious pace, jaw clenched, eyes dark. Tension hung between them like a black curtain.

It was afternoon when the wind picked up and Kate took stock of the pile of oysters and judged it to be a fair catch. She stopped working and looked at Jim, waiting for his reaction. When he turned around with another load and dumped it on the board, he caught her eye and glanced at the oysters. He nodded, and Kate dusted off her hands. At that moment a blast of wind shook the skiff, and Kate looked around anxiously. She hadn't noticed the gathering storm, and now it was almost upon them. When she looked at Jim, he was scanning the sky with a worried frown. "We'd better get out of here," he said quickly. Kate nodded. She was still wearing the oilskin apron as they hurriedly cleared off the deck.

Another furious gust of wind rocked the skiff, and Kate shivered as the icy fingers of the blast penetrated her coat. She was moving as fast as she could to prepare to leave, but the wind was increasing every second, and now the dark sky was spitting snowflakes that did a frenzied dance on the wind.

Kate rushed to the engine and tried to start it, but it wouldn't turn over. She tried again, the wind rocking her, but still the engine wouldn't come to life. After several more agitated attempts, she was cursing her luck.

"Let me try," Jim called over the wind that now howled around them. As Kate stepped backwards to give him room, the wind suddenly shook the skiff with renewed fury. The boat rocked violently, and Kate lost her balance.

She felt the railing behind her legs, and for one terrifying moment time seemed suspended as she tried futilely to regain her footing. Then she was falling backwards, her hands clutching desperately at the air, her mouth opening in a soundless scream. Her heart had stopped, and the only thought that broke through her overwhelming fear was that she was falling into her own grave.

The shock of the icy water closing over her head went straight through her bones, nearly paralyzing her. She was frozen in a nightmare colder and more terrifying than anything she'd ever known.

She struggled frantically to get her head above the surface of the water. She managed to break free once and took a great gulp of air, shaking uncontrollably and coughing. Choppy waves smacked her face, and she drew in a gulp of water with the next breath. Choking, she felt herself being dragged down again by the weight of her clothing — the work boots and heavy apron were like lead in the water. Just before she went under again she heard Jim's voice shouting her name above the storm. The sound gave her renewed strength, and she struggled toward the surface again. As her head broke free, she caught a glimpse of his face, and it seemed demonic in its intensity. He was leaning far over the side of the boat, and it flashed through her numbed brain that he, too, could fall in and be killed.

Kate thrashed to stay above water, but already the icy cold was taking its toll. Her arms and legs had little feeling, and she struggled to make them move. Her muscles were slow to respond, and even her thoughts seemed to slow down. "Grab my hand!" Jim shouted above the roar of the wind, but though she tried to reach out, she couldn't seem to make her arm work.

She was sinking again, being pulled down inexorably to the depths, and she hadn't the strength to fight it. She'd never see Jim again, she thought with an intolerable ache. "Kate!" His voice was agony itself, and she had a fleeting glimpse of him beginning to climb over the side of the boat. Dear God! He was coming in after her!

She forced her head above water and exercised every last ounce of strength to reach out. She couldn't see anymore as the wind whipped her soaked hair across her face, and it seemed that her arm grasped at empty air forever while she desperately tried not to go under again. Her little remaining strength was ebbing fast. Just when she thought she wouldn't last another second, she felt his hand clasp her wrist. She was dragged closer to the boat, and then he was pulling her up by her arm. The wind whipped around her violently as he dragged her from the water, but she hardly felt it. She was numb all over. Even her blood was like an icy river.

He pulled her halfway onto the boat, and then his arms grasped her waist, and she felt herself hoisted onto the deck and cradled against him. She forced her head back to look into the face she'd feared she'd never see again, and then she started crying. Jim was ashen, his eyes riveted on her, his hands moving over her as though she'd slip away if he let her go. He helped her to the cabin and set her down on the bench in front of the stove.

Moving rapidly, he turned on the stove and opened its door, then knelt in front of Kate and began pulling off the work boots. Every other second he'd glance up at her face, blinking hard, obviously gripped by the same stark terror as she was.

She was sobbing now, her breath coming in ragged gasps. Uncontrollable shivers racked her body, each spasm stronger than the last. "Jim," she cried as another wave of fear swept over her.

"You're safe now, honey," he rasped out hoarsely, his fingers trembling as he smoothed the wet hair from her face in a comforting gesture. He pulled the oilskin apron from her and began undressing her with shaking hands. She tried to help him peel off her icy clothes, but her fingers were numb and useless. He tugged down her jeans while her tears fell on his hair, and he murmured soft words of assurance as he worked on her shirt.

A strong blast of wind shook the boat, and the floor pitched under them. Jim stumbled against Kate, and she clutched him to her as her body trembled in fresh terror. "It's all right, honey," he whispered soothingly. "I'll get you a blanket."

He wrapped her tenderly, then rummaged in the cupboard until he found a bottle of whiskey. He curved her fingers around the glass and stroked her hair again as she took a gulp of the fiery liquid. She began coughing, but thankfully the tears stopped.

"I've got to get us out of this storm," he said, and the urgency in his voice penetrated her numb brain. She nodded, and he disappeared out the door. It took all of her strength just to wait alone while he was gone.

She heard the engine finally sputter to life, and the skiff began moving toward the shoreline, barely visible in the gathering darkness and swirling snow. She couldn't discern any landmarks through the window, but she calculated that he'd taken them somewhere near Horn Point, where he secured the craft. They were in a sheltered cove with a sheer, high bank on one side that provided protection from the furious wind. The boat rocked, but the pitching and yawing had lessened. If they could weather it out, everything would be all right.

Kate kept repeating that to herself until Jim came back into the cabin, an icy gust of wind rushing in before he shut the door. She couldn't tear her eyes away from him as he turned on a small, battery-operated lantern, its yellow glow warming the room.

He took off his coat, speaking conversationally as he moved to the marine radio. "I'd better let someone know what happened to us."

The radio crackled after Jim's call, and then a man answered. Jim explained that they'd had engine trouble but were safe. The man promised to relay the message to Tilghman Island.

Jim returned to Kate, surveying her worriedly. "Are you all right?"

"I was terrified the whole time you were outside." She laughed hollowly. "Can you imagine that? Me, the toughest woman on the bay, frightened to be alone."

Jim knelt slowly and took her hand in his. "I'm with you now," he whispered gently.

"I never knew what real fear was, not until I fell overboard. I thought I'd never see you again."

He lowered his head and pressed her hand to his lips. "I'd never let anything happen to you, Kate." He shuddered, then raised his head to look deep into her eyes, his expression still haunted. He spoke with difficulty. "Seeing you fall into the water, I knew I was watching my own life slip away. If I lost you, I lost everything that was worth a damn."

She pressed her fingers to his lips to silence him, overcome by his confession. "I nearly drowned," she cried, the horror bringing tears to her eyes. "Jim . . ." Her voice broke.

His arms went around her, and he rained kisses of solace on her hair and face. "I know, Kate," he groaned. "I know." He stood up, dragging her to her feet as he pulled her against him.

His lips found hers, and they kissed hungrily, over and over again, each murmuring the other's name, a desperate need overcoming both of them. Kate's hands were shaking as she fumbled with the buttons of his shirt, and he helped her, his hands trembling as well. Her blanket slid to the floor, and she heard his soft groan of desire. He kicked off his shoes and then stripped away the last of his clothing. He stood before her naked, the lamplight gilding his body. She reached out her hand and pressed it to his chest, then let it glide over his ribs and flat

178

stomach, communicating her need.

His breathing was as ragged as her own as he led her to the small bed against the wall.

She lay down on the mattress, and he knelt beside her, cupping her face in his hands as he kissed her with a feverish tenderness. She had never been so overwhelmed by need. She had never responded so unreservedly. "I want you so much," she cried.

She met his lips kiss for kiss with so much unbridled passion. Her mouth parted beneath his, allowing him free rein to plunder her senses. She was reeling with desire when his mouth began a slow descent from her lips to her throat and then to the creamy white skin of her breasts. He feasted his eyes on her body. Kate looked back at him, silently begging, for the touch of his lips and hands. She must have moaned her need, because he murmured, "Soon, darling, soon," in a voice raspy with hunger.

He lay down beside her, his hands caressing her at will. Heat surged through her body, a hot trail of fire covering her skin wherever he stroked.

His mouth moved to her collarbone, nibbling at the hollow there, then he trailed kisses lower, making slow circles on her breasts with his lips and tongue. Kate groaned and tangled her hands in his hair, her palm brushing the prickly hairs on his neck.

He was alternately sucking and nibbling, driving her wild with desire. She slid her hands to his shoulders and back, kneading the firm muscles there and marveling at the gentleness of his hard, lean body.

He moved so that he lay across her, and his hand stroked her hip, circling intimately around her thigh until she gasped in pleasure. She ran her hands over his back, and he groaned her name in response.

She wanted him as she had never wanted anyone in her life. She gasped in mounting excitement, and he moved his body over hers to give her what she craved, the hard promise of ecstasy.

She was more than ready for him as he parted her thighs with his knee, and she arched against him as the driving pleasure began. His soft, matted chest hair pressed against her as he moved, and she arched against him. He slipped one hand between them and ran caressing fingers over her stomach and hips, making her moan in piercing excitement. She was entirely his now, her passion unleashed and utterly in his control.

He explored her reactions intimately,

learning which caresses excited her the most, then using them to drive her to the edge of madness. He discovered that the play of his tongue on her nipples made her writhe, and a gentle caress on her thigh elicited a moan. Then he used his knowledge to torment her with sweet passion, driving her to the brink. But when her breathing quickened and her hands clutched him tighter, he stopped. Though she arched against him, he waited. "Not yet, my love," he whispered raggedly, stroking her hair.

When he gauged that she was ready, he began the caresses again, increasing the intensity. Her every nerve was begging for his touch, but he increased her frustration by playing with her, raining soft kisses on her face and throat, but refusing to deepen his kiss, and trailing his fingers over her body so lightly that she shivered for more.

Again he stopped when she thought she could endure no more, then he buried his mouth against her throat. He showed her new delights as his teeth nipped at her earlobes and neck, and then his mouth administered comfort to her raw nerves.

"You have the most beautiful long legs," he whispered to her, his hand roving down them, sending delicious shivers coursing through her.

Now the union of their bodies was too compelling to resist, and she surrendered to the passion that exploded inside her. The snowstorm raged outside, but inside the cabin it was all heat as though the sun had exploded, sending millions of white-hot shards into her flesh.

She was breathing in shallow gasps as the waves of passion gradually receded. He smoothed the hair from her face, kissing her deeply. His breathing matched her own. He cradled her head to his shoulder, then pulled the blanket over both of them. Kate turned her face to his neck and buried her lips there, exhausted by their lovemaking. She had never truly been made love to before — with Jeffrey it had been a mechanical act, devoid of real emotion. With Jim, she had learned that there were undreamed of dimensions of pleasure — and love.

"I could stay in your arms like this forever," she breathed.

"We have forever," he answered, and she smiled as she drifted off to sleep.

chapter

8

They were still curled closely together the next morning when Kate woke up. The wind was still howling around the cabin, rocking the boat. She stirred slightly, and the hand around her waist tightened. "Good morning, my love," Jim whispered against her ear, his breath warm.

"Good morning, darling." She turned in his embrace to face him, smiling sleepily. "I feel wonderful this morning, with an appetite like a horse. How would you like some pancakes for breakfast?"

"I can think of something better to satisfy my hunger at the moment." He laughed softly, pulling her against him, his hands moving down her back with an urgency that made her arch toward him. He nibbled her ear, sending shivers of pleasure down her spine, and she laughed shakily.

"Suddenly I've forgotten all about pancakes," she murmured.

"Good, because I've got something else in

mind." His right arm was cradling her head, and his hand twined in her hair, holding her still, while his left hand intimately explored her naked form beneath the blanket. His fingers circled and brushed her nipples until they hardened in response. She strained against him, wanting the feel of his body on hers, but he wouldn't let her touch him. One leg held hers steady while his hand moved down over her taut stomach to stroke her hips in a sensual caress that made her writhe. His thumb traced lazy circles that widened until he reached her upper thighs.

"Jim," she gasped, her breathing becoming labored as his fingers began a more intimate exploration. She clutched his shoulders. "What you do to me," she groaned helplessly.

"And you to me," he murmured, his eyes intense with passion as they swept over her flushed face. "How I've wanted you, Kate. More than you can know."

"I think I *do* know," she teased him in a shaky whisper. "You made it pretty clear on several occasions."

"I wanted you to be sure, Kate, sure that you wanted me as much as I want you."

"I do," she said, her breath quickening again as his caresses sent her spiraling out of control.

"Hasn't anyone ever made love to you properly?" he demanded with a mock growl.

She shook her head, almost unable to speak because of the rising tide of passion. "Never," she whispered brokenly. "Never like this."

He was silent for a moment, his eyes filled with such incredible tenderness that she wanted to cry. "It was never like this for me either," he whispered.

His mouth lowered to her throat, and his lips and tongue played with alternating gentleness and savagery until a hoarse cry of mindless pleasure escaped her. She touched his back, his hips, and thighs, stroking the corded muscles with abandon, her excitement growing with each muffled groan he made against her skin.

She was eager for their joining, her body agonizing for the pleasure he gave her. Her naturally seductive movements aroused him as much as her caresses, and they matched each other in the intensity of the passion they gave. And in the exquisite moment of love, when sensation blocked out the rest of the world, she knew that this was a gift they gave each other, a gift that was theirs alone to share.

"I love you," she cried hoarsely, drowning in love, and he expelled his breath in a ragged sigh of release as his body shuddered with hers.

"I love you too, Kate," he murmured hoarsely against her throat, and he clutched her to him.

They must have slept afterwards because Kate blinked to see that a patch of sunlight shone through the cabin window. She stretched her legs slowly and turned her head to find Jim watching her with a lazy smile. He cradled her tighter against him and murmured her name gently.

"Storm's over," she whispered, and he sighed.

"Too bad," he said softly.

"Yes," she agreed with a smile. "Too bad." She traced a line over his jaw teasingly, and Jim turned her palm up to kiss it. "It must be true what they say about oysters being an aphrodisiac." She laughed, her eyes bright with happiness.

He grinned back at her. "Come here, Captain Kate," he threatened her teasingly, "and I'll show you how true it is."

She was all too willing and curved her body compliantly against his, leaning over him on her elbows. He cupped her face in his hands, then pulled her head down for a hungry kiss. "My beautiful Kate," he mur-

186

mured against her lips. "My beautiful, beautiful Kate."

She rolled to his side, sighing, and brushed his chest with her hand. "I love the way you say my name."

"Kate, Kate, Kate," he murmured, giving her a kiss each time he said it. "And there are a million more where those came from." He smiled.

Her eyes softened as she looked at him. "I never knew I wasn't a whole person," she whispered. "I let myself be used once in the guise of love, and I didn't even know it."

Jim regarded her with tender sympathy and gently stroked her cheek. Then he gave her a mock leer and said in a theatrical voice, "Ah, my dear, but I intend to use your body again and again."

He pulled her to him and kissed her deeply, and when he lifted his mouth from hers, Kate looked into his eyes and drawled lazily, "What a horrible fate."

They were still kissing when they heard the sound of an engine outside and a voice calling out. "Halloo! Anybody on board?"

Jim cursed softly and reached for his pants. "Paradise lost," he said with a wry grimace. She covered herself with the blanket while he dressed quickly. He went outside and she heard him talking to someone on another boat.

"Picked up your call on the radio last night, buddy," a man hollered. "Live right close, so thought I'd take a run out this mornin' and check on your location. You okay?"

"Just fine," Jim called back. "Thanks a lot. Guess we'll be heading back now that the wind's died down."

"Right. Take care now. Quite a storm we had last night. Early for snow. Well, be seeing you."

"Thanks again," Jim called, and Kate heard the other boat leave. He came back in and shut the door, rubbing his hands together. "It's cold out there this morning." He looked down at her wrapped in the blanket and gave a sigh of regret. "I guess we really will have to start back. Other boats are liable to start looking for us. It's beautiful out, Kate. Quiet, peaceful. Just a dappling of snow on the shore. It's hard to believe there was such a storm last night."

> *"Often 'tis in such gentle temper found,*
> *That scarcely will the very smallest shell*
> *Be mov'd for days from where*
> * it sometime fell,*
> *When last the winds of Heaven were*
> * unbound."*

She stopped reciting and looked at him with a smile.

"Byron?" he asked with a frown. Then he snapped his fingers. "No, no. Keats."

"That's right," she cried in delight. "How did you know?"

"I took a liberal dose of poetry in college. Keats was one of my favorites. And you?"

"I collect poems the way some people collect seashells. That one about the sea is one of my favorites." She stood up wrapped in the blanket and began to put on her clothes, now dried by the oven, while Jim leaned back and watched with undisguised pleasure.

She bent to pick up her shirt, and the blanket fell to the floor, leaving her naked. From his vantage point, he called softly, "I praise the gods that Aphrodite, last night, was left without a nightie."

She laughed and hitched up the blanket, shooting him a mock frown. "More poetry? Not Keats, surely."

"Pure, unadulterated Carlisle. Would you like to hear a limerick I picked up in the boys' locker room in high school?"

"Not this early in the morning," she protested with a laugh, dressing quickly in the chill air. "How about some coffee instead?"

"Coming right up." He moved to the

stove and said over his shoulder, "But you definitely should have a poem written for you. Let's see now." He was talking quietly to himself while he made the coffee, and Kate smiled. Waking up in the morning with Jim was decidedly nice, something she would like to do every day of her life. Hold on, she told herself. You're casting off before the anchor's raised, as Buck would say.

But Jim had said he loved her, hadn't he? After all, she wasn't spinning dreams from clouds. Or was she? She pulled some cookies from the cupboard and set them on the table, then sat down while Jim poured the coffee.

"Coffee and poetry are served," he announced.

Kate looked up quizzically. "What?"

He set a cup before her. "Here's the coffee. Now for the poetry." He assumed a dramatic stance, his mug raised, a stern frown on his brow, and began reciting in stentorian tones.

"I've known a young lady of late,
Whose palate is far from sedate.
By men she's been wooed,
But she prefers junk food.
And that's why she's called Tasty Kate."

Kate exploded in laughter as he concluded and saluted her with his coffee mug. "You're outrageous!" she cried, still laughing. "How did you come up with that?"

Jim grinned and sat down. "I fill the tedious hours of business meetings by writing limericks about the other businessmen. They think I'm busy taking notes when I'm actually immortalizing them in verse. It passes the time nicely."

"A strange hobby for a high-powered businessman," she commented lightly. "This isn't a family hobby, is it?"

"Afraid not," he said, shaking his head ruefully. "My uncle doesn't indulge in anything that doesn't make money, conserve money, or invest money."

She was about to comment on his lack of enthusiasm for the business when she heard another motor outside and a voice called, "*Kathryn D*! You folks okay?"

She and Jim went out on deck together and waved to the boat, another tonging skiff. "We're fine," Kate called over the noise of the engine.

The man and woman on board waved back, then headed back down river toward the bay. Probably on their way to a morning of tonging together, Kate thought. Sometimes couples worked together, the man tonging while the woman culled.

"I suppose we should get going," she said reluctantly. "All of Tilghman Island will be out searching for us soon."

She looked out over the water, which appeared so calm and innocent now, and an involuntary shudder went through her. "When I think about yesterday . . ." she began in a soft voice, shaking her head. "I guess I have a different feeling about the bay now."

Jim nodded, and his arm went around her waist. "Respect it, Kate. But don't be afraid."

She leaned against him, feeling liquid heat radiate from his fingers, warming her blood. The bay seemed more beautiful than ever, the air crisper, and Jim's touch more fiery. She realized her brush with disaster had given her a keener appreciation of the world around her and what it offered — both good and bad.

With a little coaxing from Jim, the engine eventually started, and Kate guided the boat back down the Choptank River to the Chesapeake.

At the dock they got into their separate cars, and Jim followed her home. She was looking forward to spending a lazy afternoon with him, her head filled with visions of a pot of hot tea, cookies, and Jim. "A jug of wine, a loaf of bread and thou," she said out loud, laughing to herself. But her visions faded when she saw the strange car parked in the driveway. Her first thought was that something had happened to Buck, and she leaped out of her car on the run.

But, to her surprise, the door opened, and Buck came hobbling out, leaning on a cane for support. Behind him stood a woman. When she stepped outside, Kate was startled to recognize Louise Andrews.

She stopped short, looking from one to the other. "I don't mind tellin' you, Kate Flannery," Buck said, limping toward her, "that last night you had me worried out of my head. But I see you two are all right."

"Your leg," Kate said, taken aback. "The cast is gone."

"Doc Broomfield took it off yesterday. Said I pestered him so much he wanted to get me off his hands. So I get home and no Katie, and then that storm comes up."

"I'm sorry," Kate said, chagrined. "If I'd known you'd be home, I would have gotten word to you."

"Never mind. Red called. It seems word got passed all over this island anyway." Jim came up to stand beside her, and Kate flushed, realizing what other news must have made the rounds, that she and Jim had spent the night together. "Poor Mrs. Andrews called me last night when the storm hit," Buck continued, "and she couldn't find Jim anywhere. I told her what happened."

Kate glanced at Louise, and her breath stopped when she saw how ashen the woman was. Louise took a tentative step forward and stared at Jim. "Are you okay?" she asked, her voice trembling, her eyes riveted to him.

"I'm fine," he assured her quietly. "We had trouble with the engine and had to make for shore. We tied up in a cove overnight."

"I thought . . . I was afraid . . ." Her voice broke, and she covered her face with her hands, her body racked with sobs. Jim was at her side in an instant, his arm around her shoulder, his voice soothing as he tried to comfort her.

Kate stood by helplessly, her heart going out to the woman. She was grateful that no one knew that she'd fallen overboard — that would only have fueled Louise's fears.

"You never should have gone out on the bay," she cried with a shudder. "You could have been killed in that storm. I warned you, but you wouldn't listen." She was shaking her head, her eyes dry now, her anger surfacing through her fear. Buck glanced at Kate, and she gave him a wry smile.

"I'm all right," Jim was saying firmly. "Now why don't you go on home and stop worrying? Everything is just fine."

"What about you?" Louise demanded.

"I'm going to stay here with Kate for a while."

Louise shook her head. "I don't want to be alone, Jim. Martin won't be back until late tonight, and I can't stand the thought of being in that house alone. Please." The terror was still in her voice, and Kate saw Jim's resolve waver, his jaw clench. He glanced at her, and she nodded in assent.

"All right," he said quietly. "I'll stay with you until Martin comes home. I don't know why Paula can't do it though."

"She's not family," Louise protested. "You are." She made an effort to collect herself. Drawing herself up to her full height, she smoothed her suit, then turned to Buck. "Thank you for your help, Mr. Flannery," she said with quiet dignity. "I think I'll be going now." Her eyes swung to Kate. "Good-bye," she said quickly, lowering her eyes. She brushed past Kate, got in her car, her face resuming its set composure.

"I'm sorry, Kate," Jim apologized as he walked over to her. "This isn't what I'd planned."

"I know," she said quietly, "but it's all right. She needs you tonight."

"How come you're so understanding?" he asked softly, his eyes warm.

"Are you sure you don't have me confused with someone else?" she asked teasingly, remembering the times they'd argued over each other's supposed lack of understanding.

Jim grinned at her and tilted up her chin with one hand, his thumb caressing her lower lip. "You know I don't want to go," he whispered in a voice intended just for her. His mouth brushed hers lightly before he gave in to a stronger hunger and deepened the kiss. Kate's lips opened in abandon, and she tangled her fingers in his hair, pulling him closer. His hand caressed her cheek as he slowly raised his mouth from hers. "See you later, love," he whispered huskily.

She gave him a lazy smile. "Good-bye, Jim."

"I'm glad you're home, Buck," he said, turning to go. "Take care of that leg."

"I will, son," Buck returned with a

friendly nod. "Maybe we can go goose hunting next Saturday morning if you're free."

"Sounds great. I'll see you then."

Kate's eyes followed Jim's departure, but her smile faded when she saw Louise Carlisle watching her with a concerned frown.

"What happened on that skiff last night?" Buck asked with a shake of his shaggy hair as they walked into the house. "No, don't answer that. Tell me what's wrong with Mrs. Andrews. Why was she so upset? She wouldn't say a word when she got here, just paced up and down like a caged tiger. Wouldn't have a cup of coffee or nothin' at all." Buck sank down wearily at the kitchen table, propping his cane against his chair.

"Jim's father drowned on the bay — he was a waterman," Kate explained. "He was her only brother. She's petrified something will happen to Jim."

"It's an awful way to go," Buck agreed, shaking his head. "I've lost friends, and every time I go out I pray it don't happen to me."

Kate shuddered, thinking how close she'd come to an icy grave. She looked at Buck, wanting to tell him what had happened, but she stopped herself. She knew he worried about her, but he was wise enough to let her live her own life. It wouldn't be fair to burden him with the knowledge that she'd almost drowned.

"She doesn't even want Jim near the bay," she said.

"She's frightened." Buck whistled. "I suppose it doesn't matter though. He's pretty well set at the refinery."

"I suppose so," Kate said, strangely disquieted. Then she thought of the lovemaking she and Jim had shared the night before and that morning, and she shook off the feeling. With a secret smile she stood up and started toward her bedroom.

"You goin' to do some readin'?" Buck asked.

"No," she grinned, "I'm going to write a limerick." She laughed at his mystified expression. "I'll fix us some lunch in a bit," she called out cheerily over her shoulder.

Kate woke up early Friday morning with a feeling of sweet expectancy. She smiled to herself in the dark, thinking what a pleasure early rising had become. It meant that she would see Jim that much sooner. She hummed quietly to herself as she got dressed, even breaking into an improvised jig as she combed her hair in front of the mirror. Her eyes fell on the top of her dresser as she spun around in a circle, dancing.

Laughing out loud, she picked up the folded piece of paper with the limerick she'd written and hurried to the kitchen, still humming under her breath. Fudge stirred from his position near the door and regarded her with both ears cocked.

"Good morning, sir," she said cheerfully. "Will you be having our Continental breakfast? A croissant? Some juice?" He tilted his head to one side, and Kate laughed. She unwrapped a butterscotch snack cake, one of Fudge's favorites, and placed it on the floor in front of him. After a tentative sniff, he gobbled down the sweet. "Now don't tell Buck," Kate warned him. "He doesn't think I should be feeding you anything but dog food."

Jamming the limerick into her coat pocket, she raced to the car, still humming. Her skin began to tingle all over even before she saw Jim waiting for her at the dock.

He was devouring her with his eyes as she approached. "Good morning, gorgeous," he growled. "Pleasant dreams?"

"You should know." She laughed. "You were in them."

They climbed on board and cast off

easily. Kate was nearly overcome with exhilaration to be on the Chesapeake this morning. She pointed excitedly to a flock of geese rising overhead from a nearby marsh.

They arrived at the oyster bar early. As soon as they were anchored Jim drew Kate into his arms and gave her a hard, demanding kiss. She murmured excitedly against his lips and clutched at his coat, her senses already drugged by sweet desire. But the sound of another boat motor made them break reluctantly away. "Not another damn tonger," he groaned in irritation as the other skiff pulled up a short distance from them and prepared to tong. "We haven't had a minute alone since that storm. Your grandfather's back home, my aunt won't give me a moment's peace, and now we're trailed everywhere by skiffs full of spies."

"They're only following us because our luck's been good lately, and we've had big catches," Kate said, unruffled.

"Then let's lead them back to the dock. We can go get breakfast, and they can try their luck elsewhere." He threw a black look toward the skiff. "Though the way things have been going they'd probably follow us right to the restaurant. Well, I suppose we should get busy. The sooner we start, the sooner we finish."

He set about tonging while Kate culled. They were joined by a total of three other skiffs that morning. Everyone worked at a polite distance of each other. Jim was more taciturn than even during the day before, and Kate watched as his frown grew more pronounced with each passing hour. Finally she suggested that they take a break, and he agreed, wiping his brow and stretching. They sat down on the deck and leaned against the side of the skiff, the silence lengthening between them. Jim seemed pensive, and Kate watched him surreptitiously, her heart thudding.

After some time she started to rise, but Jim caught her hand and pulled her back down beside him. "Kate, I want to talk to you," he said quietly. She waited, her breath suspended, as she noted the intensity of pain on his face. "It's about Leora," he said quietly. Kate felt a knot in her throat, half dreading what he might say. "She's been on my mind a lot lately," he said quietly, his voice faltering slightly.

But before he could say anything else an oyster shell came sailing across the water from another skiff and landed at their feet with a clatter. It was quickly followed by hoots of laughter from the other boats and another bombing of shells. "You two are supposed to be tongin', not cuddlin'," a rough, teasing voice shouted across the water. Kate scrambled quickly to her feet, her face flushed. Jim followed more slowly, an eyebrow cocked wryly at the intruders.

"If you paid more attention to tonging and less to us, you'd catch more," Kate hurled across to her tormentors, bending down and sending a shell back to its point of origin.

The tongers laughed good-naturedly, and Kate turned to Jim. "Want to call it quits for today?"

He nodded wearily, and without speaking they got the skiff ready to turn back. When the engine started, there was more shouting from the other skiffs, remarks to the effect that they couldn't have reached their limit with as little tonging as they'd done, and what was the real reason they'd brought the skiff out — to neck like a couple of teen-agers?

Kate disregarded the teasing, glancing at Jim to find him absorbed in thought as he cleaned up the deck. Immediately she wondered what he had been about to tell her concerning Leora, and she frowned as she guided the *Kathryn D* back toward the dock.

When they arrived there was a message from Buck that Jim's uncle wanted to see him immediately. Kate gave a sigh of disappointment. There'd be no time alone that night.

"I've got to go," Jim said wearily, running his hand through his hair. "And this is my last day of vacation." Kate felt a sudden sickening lurch in her stomach. She'd forgotten about that. "Kate, I want you to promise me you won't go out on the skiff alone. Please." He gripped her arms, and there was a darkness to his eyes she hadn't often seen. She searched his face, wanting some reassurance that everything between them was as it had been the night they'd made love during the storm. But she saw only exhaustion and a strained tension on his features. Was Leora's memory coming between them, she wondered with vague uneasiness.

"All right," she said quietly, giving him a wan smile. "I'm sure Buck will be ready to tong by next week anyway."

"Good." But the hard lines on his face did not relax. It was as though only a small part of his worries had been resolved. "I'll see you whenever I can, Kate. I don't know how soon it will be, but . . ." He frowned and left the sentence unfinished. " 'Bye, Kate." He gave her a light kiss on the cheek, and then he was swinging into the white Porsche.

Kate stared after him, wondering if she had just been gently dumped. The possibility sent a surge of pain knifing through her, and she hugged her arms to herself.

She was settled comfortably in front of the TV that night with her dinner when the news story came on about Carlisle Refineries. There were sharp criticisms from the Coast Guard and from some local officials that Carlisle was dragging its heels on cleaning up the oil spill. Now there were publicly expressed fears that the problem would not be resolved.

"Martin Andrews refused to comment on the allegations," the newscaster said, "and when we contacted his office today, we were told that he was in conference and would not have a statement." A profile of Andrews followed including facts about his schooling, experience, and past environmental record, which was not unblemished. Kate felt more despondent by the moment. She froze when a file picture of Jim came on the screen. "Andrews's nephew, Jim Carlisle, is considered to be second-in-command at the refinery, but he too could not be reached today for comment," the newscaster said. "Carlisle holds the title of petroleum engineer, but he's rumored to be next in line for Andrews's position when the chairman of the board retires."

The newscaster went on to profile Jim, and Kate felt every word hit her like a shower of ice crystals. "His marriage to socialite Leora Mason was brief and ended in tragedy when his young bride was killed in a car accident. Intimate friends say he's never recovered from that loss. Time will tell whether he will continue his uncle's policies at Carlisle and what direction our area's largest employer will take in the future." Kate found herself still staring at the screen, absorbed in thought, after the story ended and a commercial came on.

She had more questions than answers. It had all been so easy and so right when she'd been in Jim's arms on the rocking boat. But now things were going sour. There was the refinery still between them like a malevolent presence. And there was Leora. Where did that leave Kate?

It was like being overtaken on the Chesapeake by a violent storm and trying futilely to outrun it. She was caught inexorably in an overpowering storm of love. But whether she survived or was cast against a rocky shore was up to fate — and Jim.

"Heaven help me," she murmured out loud, still stunned.

chapter

9

Kate bit back a cough as she stared out the slats of the duck blind on the bay. Jim kept throwing concerned glances her way, but she pretended to be engrossed in her gun.

After a long week without him, punctuated only by the nightly phone calls that left her wanting him more than ever, it was finally Saturday morning, and they were hunting.

But Kate had awakened with a scratchy, raw throat, a throbbing headache, and a stomach that rolled alarmingly at the mere thought of food. She strongly suspected that she was coming down with the flu, but she didn't want Jim and Buck to cancel their outing on her account. She had a selfish reason as well. She needed to see Jim and reassure herself that everything was still all right between them. His phone calls had been short because he was working every night at the refinery. He sounded tired, and Kate couldn't help worrying that he was calling only because of a sense of responsibility toward her.

Buck murmured excitedly, and Kate looked up to see him pointing through a slat. She followed the direction of his hand and saw the familiar V formation of the Canada geese and caught the first sound of distant honking. Immediately Buck raised the goose call to his mouth and began the mournful cry. The leader dipped down toward the marsh, hesitant but interested, and Buck continued the call. An answering call came from the lead goose, who began to descend toward the decoys.

"Keep comin', friend," Buck whispered patiently, then he gave another call. The goose answered, and the rest of the V formation followed him in for a landing.

"Okay," Buck said when the geese, about ten of them, had begun to touch down on the water against the wind. All three hunters raised their guns to the slats, and Buck squeezed off the first shot, Jim the second. Kate's twelve-gauge felt like a lead weight, but she managed to brace it against her shoulder and sight one of the geese as the flock exploded into the air, startled by the loud reports. She squeezed off a shot, then felt a wave of nausea ripple through her and quickly lowered the gun again.

"Kate!" Jim's voice was sharp, and she looked at him through glassy eyes. Then she realized she had slumped forward and that the gun was resting on the floor.

Fudge had raced out to the water at the first shot, and as the rest of the geese continued their upward flight with a frantic beating of wings, the dog plowed through the marshy water to retrieve the fallen birds.

Kate heard Jim say her name again, but she barely understood as she groped her way to the open back of the blind. Her pulse was beating frantically, and her stomach gave another lurch. She half-collapsed to her knees on the ground, and then she threw up, clutching her stomach as another spasm shook her.

In an instant Jim was beside her, stroking her hair. She gave him a weak smile. "Sorry," she murmured.

"You're burning up with fever," he said in alarm as he pressed his hand to her forehead. It felt so cool and soothing that she just wanted to be held like that. "Come on, honey," he said gently. "We've got to get you home."

Buck was in front of her then as Jim helped her to her feet. He frowned in consternation. "You sick, Katie?"

"It's nothing," she murmured. "I'll be all

right. Why don't we go back in the blind?"

Jim shook his head adamantly, and Buck caught his eye and nodded. Kate felt bad about ruining their day. Jim wrapped his arm around her waist to support her, and she leaned on him as he helped her in to the boat.

Buck gathered up the guns and decoys and the three geese they'd shot. Fudge looked on with obvious puzzlement, but at Buck's command he jumped into the boat with them.

Kate was shaking uncontrollably with chills, and Jim pulled her against him, cradling her head on his shoulder and stroking her hair. "I'm sorry," she began murmuring in distraction.

"There's nothing to be sorry about," he said in a soothing voice.

"I ruined the hunt," she protested.

"We each got a goose," he said. "More than that would be a waste."

By the time they got back to the pickup, Kate was trembling so violently that she could hardly walk, and chills racked her body. She was barely aware that the truck had stopped when they reached the house, and Jim swung her up into his arms. She protested feebly, but he was already striding toward the door with her. He took her straight to her bedroom while Buck called the doctor, and he set her down on the edge of the bed. He found a warm nightgown in one of her drawers and handed it to her, his voice gentle as he said, "In deference to your grandfather's presence, you're going to have to undress yourself. I'll wait outside." She smiled, wishing they were alone, and set about the task with weary fingers while Jim waited in the hall.

When she was in bed with the covers pulled up, she called out a weak, "Okay," and both Jim and Buck came in. "Doctor says it's the flu goin' around," Buck said. "He's sendin' over some medicine."

She nodded, then a feeling of consternation overcame her as her stomach lurched again. "Oh, no," she managed to cry as she staggered to her feet. Jim helped her to the bathroom and held her head as she was sick again. She was too wrung out to feel embarrassed.

When she was back in bed, Jim got a washcloth and sponged off her forehead, his fingers brushing back her hair. The medicine arrived a while later, and Jim propped her up, putting two of the pills in her mouth and holding the glass of water for her. She felt drowsy after that, and fell asleep shortly, her hand holding his tightly.

She slept fitfully, her dreams distorted and strange. Jim was in all of them, but he was always just out of reach. She'd run after him only to have him disappear in a crowd. And when she thought she'd found him again, she'd call his name, only to have the woman beside him turn around, a cold smile on her face. And then an icy hand would squeeze Kate's heart. It was Leora, and her arm was linked with Jim's. He was smiling too, but he was looking at Leora. Kate begged him to look at her just once. Finally he did, the same smile on his face, but he said Leora's name. Kate died inside as they turned and walked away together.

She woke up abruptly, breathing hard, and heard Jim's worried voice. "It's all right, Kate," he murmured. "I'm right here." The room was dark, and for a minute she didn't remember where she was or why Jim was there. Then it came back to her — she was sick. She looked at him, sitting on her bed, and he bent over her, a soothing hand caressing her hair. She was holding tightly to his other hand, and he smiled at her. "It's all right," he said again. "You were calling my name. Now go back to sleep. I won't leave."

There was soft light in the room when she woke up again, and she blinked hard, her eyes hurting. Daylight was coming through her window, late morning light if she was any judge. Her eyes swept the room, taking in the glass of water on her nightstand, the bottle of medicine beside it, the basin with a washcloth, and an empty coffee cup. She was glad to be awake and feeling much better.

She flushed with warmth when she saw Jim asleep in the rocking chair in the corner.

He shifted his position, obviously uncomfortable in the hard chair, then slowly stretched, his eyes still closed. She watched lovingly as the long, trim legs extended, arms over his head, then his eyes opened slowly and moved immediately to her face. A slow smile warmed his eyes. "You're awake?" he asked softly.

She nodded. "And feeling much better. I must have slept all day."

He stood up and came over to her, sitting down in the chair by the bed. "Two days, actually," he said quietly, and she widened her eyes in disbelief. "Today's Monday," he confirmed.

"You haven't been here all this time?" she protested in distress, noting how tired and drawn he appeared. He couldn't have gotten more than a couple of hours of sleep.

"It's all right," he said easily. "I caught

some sleep in the chair."

"You must have hardly slept at all," she said. "Where's Buck?"

"He went out dredging with Red today. I figured he'd be all right with a whole crew on the boat."

"You're exhausted," she said.

"I'll rest up later. Do you think you'll be all right by yourself until Buck gets home? I've got to get back to the refinery."

"Sure. Don't worry."

"Buck asked Mary to look in on you today. I hate to leave you like this, honey, but there are a lot of things I've got to do." He stretched slowly and raked one hand through his hair. "Are you sure you'll be okay?"

She smiled in reassurance, and Jim came to the bed, bent down, and kissed her lightly. Kate murmured her dissatisfaction, but he stood up. "When you're better," he promised.

"I'll make the fastest recovery on record."

When he'd gone, Kate navigated carefully to the kitchen and made some toast.

Someone knocked on the door, and she called, "Come on in, Mary. It's open."

She was caught totally by surprise when she turned from the sink and saw Louise Andrews standing just inside the door. She recovered quickly. "Come in," she said politely. "I'm sorry I'm not dressed yet."

"That's quite all right," Louise said, closing the door. "I know you haven't been well. I was wondering if you felt up to having a little talk today." She was still standing in front of the door, her beige skirt and jacket neat and official, her black purse clutched tightly over her stomach. Distracted, Kate saw that her knuckles were white with tension.

"Yes," Kate said quietly. "Please sit down."

Louise moved to the table and sat rigidly while Kate pulled the lapels of her robe closed over her nightgown. As she sat down opposite the woman, she felt a pang of foreboding when she saw the shadows in Louise's eyes.

"Jim called Martin yesterday," Louise said with a polite smile. "He said you had the flu and that he was going to stay here for a couple of days."

"Yes, he was very kind," Kate said, certain that this idle exchange of pleasantries was only the preliminary. "He went back to work today. I hope he won't be snowed under because he missed a day."

Louise lifted her eyebrows expressively. "He has all that business with the spill. I'm afraid it's one giant headache. The environmentalists won't leave him alone."

Not wanting to argue, Kate said, "I thought Jim was in favor of pollution control. He said he was trying to implement some of his ideas."

Louise laughed shortly. "My dear, you haven't been around the business as many years as I have. Martin tells anyone who will listen, especially the press, that he's all for environmental protection. But away from the public he complains that environmental protection is another word for government interference. I'm afraid that's one of the sad facts of private enterprise."

"But surely Jim doesn't share those views," Kate said, shocked.

Louise gave her an indulgent smile. "Jim will be appointed to the board of directors very soon. And then he'll be in line for the chairmanship of the board. If he values his job, he'll echo Martin's views on the role of the refinery. The rest of the board won't stand for any moderation of current policy."

Kate's throat constricted, and she couldn't speak.

Louise smiled without humor. "The business is Martin's life. He lives and breathes it. Therefore, so do I. Are you prepared to do that as well?"

Kate was momentarily startled, and she couldn't phrase an answer. "I don't know if I could become that immersed in it," she said honestly.

"That's what I was afraid of." Louise's eyes hardened. "I can tell that Jim is getting involved with you, is serious, and frankly I'm not happy about it. You know my views about the bay — I don't ever want Jim doing what his father did. Therefore, I want to know what your plans are. Would you give up this life and devote yourself to the family business?"

Kate flushed, angered at the woman's blunt interference. "I think that's up to Jim to ask," she said quietly.

"He wouldn't," Louise said immediately. "Surely you know he will say that he accepts you for what you are. But think ahead. Would you give this up for him and be the kind of wife he needs, a wife like Leora?"

Kate flinched, then floundered for an answer. "He's never told me about her," she said at last.

Louise took a deep breath, a triumphant gleam in her eye. "I'm not surprised," she said quietly. "Leora was a lovely girl. She was every mother's dream. Jim's mother was quite fond of her." Louise smiled in memory. "She loved clothes and had quite a flair for fashion. They made such a handsome couple. Leora was brought up among the social elite, and she handled herself beautifully. She had a wonderful coming out party — of course that was some time before she and Jim became serious. She never seemed ready to settle down until she met him." Louise's eyes were dreamy as she said, "The wedding was one of the most beautiful I've ever seen."

She paused, and Kate said hesitantly, "They moved to California, didn't they?"

"Yes. They honeymooned there, and Leora fell in love with it. I can't blame her. Carlisle Refineries has some West Coast shipping offices, and Jim joined them." A cloud seemed to settle over Louise's features. "It was so awful when we heard about the accident. I don't think Jim's ever gotten over it."

Kate swallowed hard. "Perhaps he's trying."

The older woman's gaze swung back to Kate. "Think hard about what you're getting into. I'm not saying this just because I don't want Jim connected with the bay. Will you really be comfortable around Jim's business acquaintances and friends? I'm afraid oyster tonging isn't much of a conversational gambit at the cocktail parties he's used to. And you'd be expected to entertain. Think hard about it, Kate. You're not born to the life Leora was, and I don't mean that as an insult. It's just a fact of life that you're from two different worlds."

Kate felt tears welling up, closing off her throat, and she didn't answer. "It wouldn't be the end of the world," Louise said, not unkindly. "We all have our love affairs that don't work out." There was a bitter smile on her face now. "Martin wasn't my first love. Drew — that was his name — and I were from different worlds, too, like you and Jim. My family wouldn't accept him. And so it ended." It seemed to take a moment for her to compose herself, then she said, "But I didn't die. The world went on. And eventually I met Martin. Believe me, Kate, you'll get over Jim."

"Provided I give him up," she said evenly.

"I think eventually you'll see that it's best for both of you," Louise said with a stiff smile, standing up and straightening her skirt. "You just have to accept that some things in this world weren't meant to be. Leora would always be between you, like a shadow."

"We'll see," Kate said, a polite smile on her face.

Louise looked at her with what appeared to be great sadness in her eyes. She nodded. "Well, I hope you feel better soon. Good-bye, Kate."

Kate closed the door after her, then leaned against it and squeezed her eyes shut to hold back the tears. Everything Louise had said came flooding in on her, and she felt overwhelmed. She couldn't give Jim up. It wasn't fair for Louise to even ask her to do that.

She stumbled back to the kitchen table and sat down, laying her head down on her arms. Why did it have to be so complicated? They were from two different worlds. She couldn't deny that, but it didn't matter. She loved Jim, and the fact that they came from diverse backgrounds didn't affect that love. Or did it? How would he feel about her in the future when he began to compare her to Leora?

Slowly Kate began to consider the awful possibility that Louise might be right. She wasn't capable of entertaining the way Leora obviously had; she couldn't begin to mix with the social crowd he would expect her to.

And what of his job? Louise had said that his position would be in jeopardy if he didn't back up his uncle in refinery policies.

Could Kate live with a man who had to sub-jugate his own beliefs to those of a board of directors? A man who was less than totally committed to his ideals? The answer was an unequivocal no, and she banged her fist on the table. Damn!

Louise was wrong! But the seeds of doubt had been sown, and they took root as the day wore on.

chapter

10

By Friday Kate had shaken off the last effects of the flu and was anxious to get back out on the bay. But Buck wouldn't hear of it, so she worked on her research projects instead. Mary had visited her twice, but still Kate was bored. And she couldn't get her mind off Jim's aunt and what she'd said. Jim and Kate, Jim and Leora, Jim and the refinery — it was all a vicious circle that kept turning in her head like some torture wheel.

Jim had called the night before, sounding tired and down, and asked Kate if she felt up to having dinner with him that night. She wanted to see him so much, to talk to him and try to sort out her feelings, and now she almost dreaded the time when they would be together. She had no idea how she was going to tell him about her doubts.

Buck was going hunting again in the morning, and he left Friday evening to spend the night at Red's so they could get an early start. When Jim arrived to pick up

Kate, she was dressed in a black skirt and a pink pullover sweater with tiny embroidered flowers all over it. "You're the best thing I've seen all week," he said with a smile. "How are you doing?"

"All recovered, thanks to the good care I got from you." She stood smiling back at him, feeling a surge of love at the sight of him. He seemed to become more handsome each time she saw him. What a difference love made. "You look tired," she said worriedly.

"It's been a hellish week," he agreed with a quick twist of his lips. The lines around his eyes had deepened, and there were shadows on his face as though he'd lost weight and slept badly. He was wearing brown slacks and a beige sweater, and his eyes seemed more intense than ever. "Would you mind if we ate at my apartment instead of going out?"

"I could cook something here if you want," she ventured.

He shook his head with a grateful smile. "I appreciate the offer, Kate, but I've already got a couple of steaks in the refrigerator. It's no trouble, really."

She agreed then, and Jim drew her into her arms, his mouth on hers in a way that made her knees weak. "Let's go," he said huskily. "It seems like forever since we've been alone."

They drove up the shore road to his apartment, but before they arrived Jim turned the Porsche toward the bay on a winding blacktopped road. Kate glanced at him curiously, but he said nothing. At length he pulled up to a crest, turned into an unpaved lane, and stopped the car. They walked hand in hand to the edge of a bluff. "How do you like it?" he asked, nodding toward the broad blue expanse of the Chesapeake just ahead of them.

"It's beautiful," she murmured. The last rays of the setting sun were drawing away from the water, leaving it a dusky orchid hue by the shore.

"This is my land," he said, gesturing around them. "My father bought it and left it to me. I'd thought of building a house here one day. Leora and I talked about it . . ." His eyes lost their luster, and he trailed off, not finishing his thought. Kate felt the same cold shiver that Leora's name always invoked, and she stared silently out at the bay. If things had been different, Jim and Leora might have had their house here. Kate felt an ache build in her throat, and she forced it back down.

"It's the perfect place for a house," she said quietly.

Jim turned and smiled at her, and her ache eased a little. "I'm glad you like it. Now let's go eat dinner."

He was quite adept at cooking steaks. Kate mixed a tossed salad for them. "You've been holding out on me," she said lightly, watching him take frozen corn from the freezer and a package of rolls from the refrigerator. "You know how to cook."

"*Au contraire,* my dear," he said with a grin. "What I do is open boxes and dump them into boiling water. That hardly constitutes cooking."

"Then we're on a par." She laughed.

"Sometime you can give me the recipe for your famous heartburn croquettes," he teased her. "I need a gourmet dinner speciality."

"Serve them only if you don't want your company to ever return," she said. "They rate right up there with creamed chipped beef on toast."

"Here," he said, handing her two plates, a steak on each. "Medium rare. I guarantee it."

He pulled a bottle of Bordeaux from the wine rack on the counter, and they sat down to eat. "To good friends," she said, holding up her glass.

His eyes grew suddenly serious as he held

up his glass. "We're more than that, aren't we, Kate?"

"Yes," she said hesitantly, her eyes wavering as she remembered Louise's warnings about the impossibility of their relationship. Her heart was pounding faster as she stared at the wineglass, knowing that Jim's warm eyes were on her. Then he reached out and a finger tilted up her chin. "I love you, Kate," he said softly.

She met his eyes then and felt a burning desire rise in her throat when she saw the glow in the hazel depths. When he looked at her like this, all of Louise's warnings went out the window. She loved him too much to ever give him up. "I love you, Jim," she said simply.

"So what do you think we should do about it?" he asked mockingly.

"I could have some handbills printed up," she said, a happy laugh bubbling up in her throat.

He smiled at her, and she smiled back, and suddenly they were both laughing. He clasped her hand across the table. Raising it to his mouth, he kissed her fingers. "Eat your dinner," he said in a soft growl. "Then we can negotiate dessert."

By the time dinner was over, dessert was the last thing on Kate's mind, and she didn't protest when Jim swung her up in his arms and headed for the bedroom. "The dishes," she murmured, but he silenced her with a kiss.

"Let the butler do them."

"Good old Jeeves." She laughed against his throat.

The bedroom was decorated in shades of brown, a plush carpet on the floor and a large bed with a bookcase-headboard against the far wall. There were more pieces from Jim's rock collection on the night table and several books. He sat down on the chenille bedspread with Kate on his lap, and pushed two books onto the floor. A quick glance told her they were engineering manuals, but she didn't dwell on that thought because he suddenly lay back, pulling her down on top of him. Then he rolled over so that he was on top, kissing her hungrily all the while. His hands slipped beneath her sweater, and she moaned in growing excitement as his fingers encountered her bare breasts. He bent his head, his mouth closing over the rounded softness, and his hands slid beneath her to unzip her skirt. Rolling to her side, he easily finished the job of stripping her and leaned on one elbow, surveying his handiwork with obvious relish.

"Now it's my turn," she breathed huskily,

and she began pulling his sweater up over his head. He lay with a satisfied grin on his face, obviously enjoying having her undress him. He shrugged the sweater all the way off, sighing as her hand caressed the mat of hair on his chest. Then she undid his belt, and soon his pants and shoes were on the floor as well.

She explored him tentatively, eliciting growls of pleasure as her hands moved over his back, chest, and down his stomach. He pulled her to him, and then the hunger between them took over. Her mouth met his in fierce demand, parting to the thrust of his tongue. He leaned over her, his lips teasing and tasting her neck and then her breasts with agonizing slowness, making her arch with a little gasp when his tongue sought her hardened nipple.

She shivered as an exquisite sensation ran through her veins, a hot narcotic that rendered her nearly immobile. Like the first time, he played with her, taking her to peaks of sensation she'd never experienced, until she dug her nails into his back. She returned his kisses in full measure, tasting the saltiness of his skin on his shoulder, his chest, his arms. Where his hands and mouth touched, her nerves flamed into such scorching sensitivity that nothing mattered but Jim and the pleasure he was giving her.

He turned her unresisting body over and administered his love play on the backs of her legs, teaching her what an erotic area they could become. Soon she was writhing beneath his fingers and mouth. She became a shell on the beach of time and he the tide, his caresses washing over her with increasing intensity.

He finally ended the sweet frustration and turned her over again, lowering his body onto hers. She was aching for their joining, and she felt a shaft of pleasure even more intense than what had come before.

Her gasps fueled their passion, attuning him to her feelings so well that she felt he was in total control of her responses. She cried out his name, her fingers tightening in his hair, and he buried himself deeply in her body, his mouth pressing against her throat as though she was life itself. Her tension reached an unbearable peak, and a singing ran through her blood, swamping her body with explosive emotion. It was an ageless song, the song of desire and passion fulfilled.

Exhausted, they fell asleep in each other's arms. Kate woke once during the night, shivering, and pulled up the extra blanket on the bed. She smoothed the covers around Jim's shoulders and lay studying his face, gently touched by moonlight. He looked strong but tender, the hard lines on his face tempered by a boyish innocence. She loved him so much. She wasn't going to think about Leora or the refinery or Louise. Not tonight. Tonight she would sleep in his arms, warm and content, having found love.

She got up early the next morning, letting him sleep, and washed the dishes from the night before. She'd slipped on one of his brown terry cloth robes, and when she tiptoed back into the bedroom he was just stirring. "Did anyone ever tell you you're beautiful in the morning?" he asked sleepily, smiling up at her.

"Fudge mentioned it once or twice," she teased.

"I knew that dog had good taste the minute I saw him." Jim laughed, sitting up. "Come here and sit by me." He pulled her to him and gave her a proper good morning kiss.

"A day without this is a day without sunshine," she murmured.

"Then let's see if I can brighten your day some more," he teased her, his lips playing lightly on her neck and collarbone. He slid the robe from her shoulders, and she moaned as his mouth and teeth nibbled her shoulders.

"Breakfast," she gasped out. "The skillet's on. It'll burn."

He released her reluctantly with a mock frown. "We can't have a burned breakfast, can we? Tell you what, I'll take a shower, then we'll eat breakfast, and then . . ." He gave her a wicked grin and got out of bed, stark naked. He grabbed another robe from the closet and headed for the bathroom, humming. Kate watched him with unabashed admiration.

She was humming herself when she returned to the kitchen. She turned the heat down under the skillet and began mixing egg and milk for French toast. There was some bacon in the refrigerator, and she put a few slices in another skillet. Everything was sizzling nicely when the phone rang. She hesitated a moment, wondering if Jim was almost finished. The water had stopped, but he must have just gotten out of the shower. The phone rang again, and from the bathroom he hollered, "Get that, will you, honey?"

She picked up the receiver with a cheery, "Hello. Carlisle residence." There was a pause, then a female voice on the other end said, "Is Jim there? This is Mariette Mason."

She recognized the name instantly, and her mouth went dry with apprehension. Leora's sister. "Just a minute," she said in a quiet voice.

Jim came out of the bathroom, tying the belt of his robe, and Kate handed him the phone, saying softly, "Mariette Mason."

She saw something flicker in his eyes, but he gave no other sign that the call bothered him. "Hello, Mariette," he said into the phone, his voice steady and polite. Kate moved about the kitchen, turning the bacon and French toast and pouring orange juice, anything to keep her occupied. She could hear Jim's answers, his polite inquiries as to how Mariette and her family were getting along. There was a long pause, then in a quiet voice he said, "It's very nice of you to invite me, but I don't think I'll be going to the Civic Society's Christmas dance this year." Kate's stomach knotted, and she turned the French toast absently. "No," he said after a pause. "That's right. I haven't gone since the year Leora and I were named king and queen of the dance." Kate's heart squeezed tightly. "All right, Mariette. It was nice talking to you too. Okay. Good-bye."

Kate turned around when he hung up and saw him staring thoughtfully at the phone. She turned off the stove. Needing to keep her hands occupied, she set the plates on the table and folded the napkins into neat triangles.

"That was Leora's sister," he said.

Kate ran her finger nervously along the back of a chair. "King and queen," she said with false brightness. "I didn't know you were royalty."

She looked up to find his eyes boring into her. "What's wrong, Kate?"

"Nothing. I certainly hope you aren't turning down these classy invitations on my account."

He was silent for a moment. When he finally spoke his voice was very controlled. "What bothers you more, Kate — the fact that I used to go to pretentious functions like the Civic Society's Christmas dance or the fact that I haven't invited *you* to any of them?"

His words carried the sting of truth, and Kate felt the blood drain from her face. "All right," she said calmly, though she was shaking inside, "why don't you take me to the parties your friends attend?"

"Because I don't go to those parties anymore," he ground out. "If it's the busy society life you want, Kate, then you've got the wrong man."

Kate shuddered under a wave of scalding

pain, as though she'd just fallen into a crater bubbling with red-hot lava. Was he telling her that she didn't measure up to Leora?

The ringing of the phone made her jump, and Jim answered it with an annoyed frown. She watched his face grow more tired as he talked, then he sighed and ran his hand through his hair. "All right, I'll be there in a little while."

He hung up and stared at the phone, deep in thought, then turned to her. "I'm sorry I was angry, Kate. This damn refinery mess has me on edge. That was Martin. I've got to leave now."

"That's all right," she said, pretending a calm she didn't feel. "I should get back home anyway."

"I'm truly sorry, Kate." Regret shone in his eyes. "Martin says the Coast Guard is swarming all over the place. There was another spill last night. It's going to be one hell of a mess now."

She swallowed hard and tightened her fingers on the chair, wondering about the spill and what Jim was going to do. "Your uncle plans to have you seated on the board of directors soon, doesn't he?" she asked suddenly.

He seemed surprised. "Yes, I suppose so. Why?"

She shrugged. "I was just curious. You'd be pretty much bound by board policies then, wouldn't you?"

Comprehension registered on his face. "You're talking about the spill, aren't you?" She nodded, and he sighed. "I can't give you any guarantees, but I've been working very hard to get the problem resolved."

Despite his reassurance, she was still plagued by a nagging doubt. Louise had said that Jim would have to conform to Martin's views, and if the past were any indication, then Jim's principles would be compromised. She knew him, yet she didn't.

"I guess I'd better go change," she said in resignation.

Jim nodded. "I'll drop you home before I run out to the refinery."

Jim was preoccupied during the drive, and Kate found herself tangled in her own thoughts. Fudge came bounding to the car when it pulled into the driveway, and Jim turned to face Kate, his hand touching her shoulder as she reached for the door handle. "Let's get away somewhere together tomorrow," he suggested. "How about it?"

"All right," she agreed with a wan smile. "Want to take the skiff out?"

"Great. I'll bring the food."

She waited a minute, wanting to say more. But when she looked at his face, she saw the exhaustion etched there and knew it wasn't the time for questions. So she just said she'd see him the next day. Jim's hand cupped her head and he drew her to him, his lips lingering on hers. Tears welled in her eyes when he raised his head, and she hurried into the house. When she was inside, she heard the Porsche drive away, and a sudden emptiness descended on her. Louise's words rang in her ears — *Leora would always be between you, like a shadow.*

She sat down in a chair at the kitchen table, scratching Fudge absently behind his ears. "Always Leora and the refinery," she muttered in a sudden surge of self-pity. "Damn them both!"

Just then there was a knock on the door, and for a hopeful moment she thought Jim might have come back. But it was Mary. Kate tried not to show her disappointment.

"I saw the car leave," Mary said tentatively. "I guess Jim was here."

Kate nodded. "Want some tea?"

Mary shook her head, chewing her lip as though there were something on her mind. Kate gestured for her to sit down, and she took the seat opposite Kate. "What's wrong?" Kate asked.

"It's the refinery," Mary began. Kate looked at her in surprise. "There are all kinds of rumors going around," Mary rushed on. "Frank's brother works there, and he says they're going to shut it down."

"That couldn't be true," Kate said immediately. "It's one of the area's largest employers."

Mary shrugged, a worried frown on her face. "That's what Frank's brother heard. He said Mr. Andrews is having all kinds of trouble with the Coast Guard and the EPA, so he's planning to just shut down the refinery." Mary hesitated, and her eyes darted to Kate. "I don't know how to say this, Kate, but could you . . . I mean since you know Jim Carlisle . . ."

"Would I ask him if it's true?" Kate said gently.

Mary nodded. "It would be so hard on Jerry if he lost his job. They have three kids. I'm sorry, Kate. I don't want to burden you with all this."

"It's okay," Kate said soothingly. "I'll ask Jim. I'm sure he'll tell me it's only a rumor."

"Thanks. You don't know how much I appreciate it. Listen, I've got to get back. I left Frank with the kids, and he wants to run some errands. I can't thank you enough."

"It's all right," Kate said. She walked Mary to the door and then watched her hurry across the field separating the two small houses.

Despite her assurances to Mary, Kate was worried. Surely the refinery wouldn't be shut down. It would be devastating to the area's economy.

Buck spent the entire day hunting, and Kate kept busy with her research, but her mind strayed. Finally she sat down in front of the TV with a pot of hot tea to see what was on the evening news, hoping for good word from the refinery. It was the lead story, but the situation wasn't good. Kate's heart began pounding when she saw Jim surrounded by TV cameras and microphones outside the building. He looked so tired and worn down, she thought helplessly.

Questions were being fired at him from all sides, and he was trying to answer them patiently, his hands jammed into the pockets of his suit coat. He must be freezing, she thought vaguely.

"What about the rumors that the refinery is going to shut down?" one reporter demanded.

Jim shook his head. "It may be necessary to close a small portion of the operation until the pollution problem is solved, but there's no basis to the rumor that the entire plant will close."

Before he'd even finished, another reporter was calling out. "What about the Coast Guard? We understand that the refinery will be fined."

"We're working with them to correct the problem," Jim said. "As of now we haven't been threatened with a fine."

"And what about charges that the spill is the result of outdated equipment?" someone else shouted out.

Jim paused, then said firmly, "It isn't always possible to keep every piece of plant equipment up to date. But we'll be replacing a great deal of it. Now if you'll excuse me, I have to meet someone."

"Just a minute, sir," another reporter called, shoving a microphone in his face. "Why isn't Mr. Andrews available for comment?"

"Mr. Andrews is very busy working on cleaning up the spill and working with the Coast Guard," Jim said, his patience obviously coming to an end. "Now excuse me." He moved quickly through the crowd of reporters, their cameras recording his lithe strides as he walked to the Porsche and got in. The news tape cut away to a shot of the reporter standing alone outside the refinery, obviously recorded some time after the interview with Jim. "Following Mr. Carlisle's comments, there was still no report from Martin Andrews. We'll try to have further word on the refinery situation later tonight."

Kate stood up and paced the room in agitation. Jim had looked so drawn with fatigue, but he'd handled himself well under the relentless questioning by the reporters.

On impulse she went to the phone and dialed his apartment. She wanted to talk to him tonight before the outing the next day. They both needed it, she was sure. She let the phone ring for a long time, but there was no answer. Finally she hung up and paced the room again. Had he gone out to eat? Surely not, as tired as he must be. She was worried now. What if he'd had a car accident? He'd been so tired, he could have easily fallen asleep at the wheel.

Her concern mounting, Kate picked up the phone, then put it down again indecisively. She walked away, intending to fix herself some dinner, but the worry wouldn't leave her alone. Giving in, she went to the phone book and looked up the number of Jim's aunt, then dialed.

The maid answered. After Kate identified herself, the woman went to get Louise. Kate could hear voices in the background and laughter, and she wondered what was happening.

"Hello?" It was Louise's voice. Kate stammered out who she was again, then asked if Jim was there.

There was a pause before Louise said, "I'm afraid he can't come to the phone right now. You see, we're having a party tonight. I'm sure you wouldn't want to disturb him."

Her voice was icy and distant, and Kate knew she had no chance of talking to Jim that night. "All right," she said quietly. "Good-bye." Just before she hung up, she heard music start in the background, loud party music, and she slammed the phone down.

What was he doing at a party at his aunt's? She paced back and forth in the kitchen, trying to come up with a logical explanation, but she could think of none. Was he really concerned about cleaning up the oil spill? If he was, he wouldn't be attending a party that night, especially after he'd just told her he didn't go to those kind of parties anymore. Maybe the truth was that he didn't take her to those kind of parties because she didn't fit in.

Everything kept coming back to what Louise had told her. Jim's life was inextricably tied up with the refinery and the memory of Leora. How could she compete with two such powerful adversaries?

chapter

11

Kate woke up Sunday morning with a dry mouth and an ache in her throat. Then she remembered the tears that couldn't be held back when she'd gotten into bed. She'd been tormented all night by visions of Jim at his aunt's party. She'd awakened briefly when Buck had come in, then drifted back into a fitful sleep.

Wearily she dragged out of bed and headed for the shower. The hot water cleared her head some, and she wandered into the kitchen, yawning. She glanced at the pile of mail she'd thrown on the table yesterday and sighed. Probably more bills.

She leafed through the envelopes — a phone bill, another insurance form for Buck's broken leg, an ad for something or other, and a white business envelope addressed to her from Wilmington, Delaware. She checked the return address. It was a school, and she opened it, wondering what it was.

She read the first sentence and suddenly remembered. She'd applied for a teaching position at the school a while back. At the time she had sent out several applications, and most hadn't been answered.

The school was interested in her, and they wanted to interview her at her earliest convenience. Kate reread the letter, then set it aside. It wasn't exactly a job on the bay, and it was a long way from Tilghman Island. But she couldn't go on tonging oysters forever. Buck had worked hard to put her through school, and she wanted to use that education. And then there was Jim. He said he loved her, but still Kate was plagued with doubts. She had an uneasy feeling, as though the shining world she and Jim had created together was threaded with cracks.

"You look like you've got the weight of the world on your shoulders," Buck said sleepily from the doorway. Kate looked up.

"Just some problems," she murmured. "How was the hunting yesterday?"

"Not too good," Buck said, yawning. "Wind changed, and they didn't land close. We finally went to the store and sat around talkin' and then ended up at Red's for cards. How was your day?"

She shrugged. "It was okay."

"You see Jim?"

"For a little while. Then he had to go back to the refinery."

"Yeah, they're sure havin' problems there. Kind of rough on him, I guess." Buck poured himself a cup of coffee and sat down. Kate watched him, thinking how good he'd always been to her, always patient, even when she was a little girl and a lot of trouble. She detected inevitable signs of age in his face. His cheeks were more hollow, and his eyebrows whiter, but his eyes still shone with a zest for life.

"I applied to a school in Wilmington," she said softly, "and they want to interview me."

Buck looked up sharply. "That's a pretty good distance."

"I know." She stared down at the table. "But I can't be an oyster tonger forever."

"Have you talked this over with Jim?"

She shook her head miserably. "We can't seem to be alone, what with everything at the refinery." She didn't add that there was more to it than that, that Jim's aunt had raised more doubts than Kate could deal with at this point, and that she was beginning to wonder if she knew Jim at all. She kept hearing the laughter and music in the background when she'd called his aunt's house the night before. The Jim she knew wouldn't go to a party when he was so concerned about the refinery trouble. Or would he? Confused, she turned her attention back to Buck. "We're going out on the skiff today."

"That'll do you both good," Buck said approvingly. "I like Jim. Take my advice, Katie, and talk to him."

She murmured noncommittally and frowned, not sure talking would really solve anything.

Her hopes plummeted again that afternoon when Jim arrived, looking preoccupied. He was wearing his black windbreaker over a sweater and jeans and had a tired smile on his face. "It was a lousy day yesterday," he said with a shake of his head, "but it sure is good to see you today, Kate."

She bit back her question about last night's party and went to get her coat. She would save the questions until they were alone.

There was a sharp chill in the air as they boarded the *Kathryn D*, and though the sky was gray and still, there was no forecast of snow. Working together silently, they started the engine and headed the skiff out onto the bay. The crisp breeze fanned Kate's hair out behind her, and she quickly pulled on her knit cap. Jim was staring out over the water, and Kate watched him, wondering what was on his mind.

They traveled south, and Kate finally turned toward the Choptank River. She brought the skiff in along the shore where the sandy beach and dried grasses stretched off endlessly. When the skiff was secured, Kate started toward the cabin, then stopped short when she saw Jim.

"What's the matter?" he asked. "You've been cool ever since we started out." He was facing her, hands on hips, and Kate stared back.

"Mary wanted me to ask you about the refinery," she said carefully. "Her brother-in-law works there, and he's afraid you're going to close."

"Nonsense." He spat out the word coldly. "There's no way my uncle will ever let that refinery close. It's his life."

"I heard you say that on TV last night," she said quietly.

"And you still thought it was a bunch of public relations garbage?" he demanded in an equally quiet voice.

Kate shook her head indecisively. "I don't know, Jim. There are so many things . . ."

"What things?" he demanded. "Dammit, Kate. Don't do this to us."

"Do what?"

"Put this distance between us. If something's bothering you, tell me."

"All right." Her voice was calm despite her racing heart. "Why did you go to a party at your aunt's last night?"

Slowly he expelled his breath. "How did you find out about that?"

"After I saw you on TV I wanted to talk, so I called your apartment. When I couldn't get you, I called your aunt."

Jim sighed and shook his head. "I might have known. I'm sorry my aunt didn't tell me you'd called, Kate. The truth is, I was dead tired and there were reporters waiting on my doorstep so I went to Louise's. Despite the party, I managed to fall asleep upstairs."

His explanation was plausible, but some perverse demon in Kate reminded her that Jim was adept at handling tricky questions. After all, he was the spokesman for Carlisle Refineries. She remembered how composed he'd appeared on television and how believable. Was it all an act?

"Come here," he said in a gentle voice, and she allowed him to pull her close against him. He stroked her hair while she rested her head on his chest. This was another talent of his — making her doubts disappear when he held her. She looked up at him and met his warm smile and felt her pulse quicken. His eyes held hers, and she knew he was remembering, just as she was . . . that night on the skiff, that night that now seemed ages ago. He pulled her into the cabin, then turned to face her.

"I want you so much, Kate," he whispered, and she trembled all over. "So much." He ran a finger down her cheek, and she was surprised to realize that he was shaking too. Desire was flaring between them, and she felt him tense. He pulled the cap from her head and ran his hand through her hair, his eyes closing as he sighed. His fingers caressed the nape of her neck, his other hand pressing her close to him at the waist. His eyes opened briefly, and she was struck by the passion in them. Then he buried his mouth against her throat, making her feverish with sensation. Her skin was on fire, and when he moved his hand inside her jacket to caress her breasts, she moaned softly.

Jim pushed the jacket off her shoulders, and his hand lifted her sweater, exposing her creamy breasts to his fingers. She gripped his shoulders and let her head fall back as he lowered his mouth to one nipple. A tide of high-voltage current swept through her, tantalizing and arousing.

Deftly he unfastened her jeans, and when they fell to the deck, he kicked them aside. Impatient, she pulled off her shoes as he began unfastening his own shirt. Kate pulled her sweater over her head, then her eyes traveled the length of his muscled frame as he shrugged out of the shirt and unbuckled his belt. He kicked off his shoes, his eyes never leaving her face, then the rest of his clothes fell to the deck, and he stepped out of them.

He was like a lean, graceful animal, she thought as a shiver of anticipation ran through her. His hazel eyes were alight with the fire of desire, and Kate couldn't tear her gaze away. Instinctively she knew her own desire for him would never truly be slaked. She'd want him again and again, no matter what. No matter about Leora or anything else. In this at least their two worlds joined in a union that defied everything else. Their love overrode all.

She lowered herself slowly onto the bed, feasting on the sight of him. He stood over her for a moment, then lay down beside her, one hand touching her in the lightest of caresses which increased her hunger for him. His mouth and hands brought her instantly to readiness for him, but he lingered with his love play, making her arch toward him again and again. Her fingers traced excited patterns on his back, reveling in the feel of his corded muscles. She stroked lightly over his hips, and he growled her name hoarsely against her ear. Her excitement mounted, knowing that he was as eager for her as she was for him.

When at last she cried out his name, sure that she would die of frustration if he prolonged her sensual ordeal any longer, he came to her, his body melding with hers urgently. A gasp escaped her, and her hands roved quickly over his back as his lithe movements brought her closer to the pinnacle. She could feel the heat from his body, and she felt that she was being consumed in a scorching fire. Surely she would be reduced to ashes by the flame of their passion. She trembled with the gift he gave her.

They lay together, his arm cradling her head, their damp flesh glistening. Jim pulled the blanket up around them and kissed her very softly on her passion-swollen lips, his thumb tenderly stroking her cheek.

She must have slept, because the next thing she knew she heard quiet rustling in the cabin and opened her eyes to find herself wrapped in the blanket, alone. She glanced around and watched him setting food on the table. He glanced over at her and immediately his eyes warmed and a smile touched his mouth. "Hungry?" he asked softly. She nodded, content and at peace.

He watched her as she pulled on the black denim slacks and pale blue sweater. She felt good dressing in front of him, enjoying the way his eyes lit with golden ardor.

"Ah, Kate," he said wickedly, "you do strange things to my appetite." She laughed, knowing exactly what he meant, and he regarded her hungrily. "To say nothing of my libido."

She stood still, mesmerized as he moved slowly toward her, and then she was in his arms again, her senses overpowered by his presence. She was breathless when he finally ended the kiss and she looked up dazedly to see his grin. "Come on, dear lady," he said. "Our picnic awaits."

They sat down to a lunch of prosciutto, wedges of Cheddar and Swiss cheese, crusty rolls, and a mixture of crisp marinated vegetables that made the perfect accompaniment. "The deli comes through again," Jim pronounced when Kate complimented him on the food. Pears and chocolate chip cookies rounded out the meal, and Kate sighed in satisfaction. "I feel that I could take on the world now," she said in obvious contentment.

"Those are the chocolate chip cookies talking," he teased her. "You're a junk food junkie."

"Mmmm." She smiled, gazing at him lazily, her chin resting on her hands. "Let's go sit up on deck a while."

He spread the blanket on the deck and they sat on it, huddling together for warmth. The winter wind blew above their heads, the side of the boat behind their backs served as a shield. Kate rested her head on Jim's shoulder, nearly lulled to sleep by the gentle rocking of the skiff. His arm around her was warm and protective, and once again she felt they were in their own world. Gray clouds scudded above them, changing shape like thick smoke.

"I think I like winter on the Chesapeake almost better than summer," he said quietly. "There's a wildness here in winter that's like you, Kate."

"Me?" she repeated in surprise. "Wild?"

He laughed huskily. "You're as wild and free as the birds that come here from Canada for the winter. I think of you as some exotic mermaid that rose from the bay."

"You certainly have your poetic side," she murmured lightly, bemused by his description of her.

"You seem to bring out whole new dimensions of me I never knew existed," he murmured, nuzzling her ear. "You're a sorceress."

She smiled and rested her head on his shoulder, content. Her nagging questions had all but disappeared.

"This is a different part of the Chesapeake," Jim mused as if to himself, and Kate listened to him drowsily, the warmth of his embrace almost lulling her to sleep. "Up north there's the part populated by the rich boaters with their yachts and floating parties, and down here there are the oystering skiffs, rich in a different way. Two different worlds."

The phrase jerked Kate back to reality, and she stiffened. The picture of Jim and Leora on the cabin cruiser flashed into her mind, and she felt as though she'd had cold water dashed on her contentment. "The other world," she began quietly, her heart beating hard. "You're a part of that, Jim."

He looked down at her, and his frown deepened as he studied her. "What are you talking about?"

She looked out over the water, averting her eyes. "You live in that world of fancy parties, yachts, and charity balls."

"I thought we went through this," he said

in a deceptively quiet voice.

His fingers tightened on her shoulder, but still she wouldn't look at him. "What else?" he asked. "Isn't there another part of that world you haven't mentioned?"

She swallowed and drew up her knees, hugging her arms around them. "The refinery," she said quietly. "It's part of that world."

His arm dropped slowly from her shoulder, and with a great sigh he levered himself up and stood looking out over the bow of the boat. The wind ruffled his windbreaker and the brown waves of his hair, making Kate very aware of him as a man. But she also felt a shiver of apprehension because it suddenly struck her that he was like no man she had ever known. She'd been off balance since the day he'd walked onto her boat.

"I owe certain loyalties," he said quietly, "and I intend to honor them as long as I'm able. I have to see things through, Kate."

She closed her eyes, trying to hold down the anguish that welled up inside her. Loyalty, she thought bitterly, was something she valued. But Jim's loyalty was to an institution she found distasteful. How could she commit herself to him? No matter how much she loved him, she couldn't live a life of hypocrisy. She couldn't go to his business functions and smile and pretend it didn't matter that the refinery was contributing to the destruction of the Chesapeake she loved so well.

Jim must have sensed her turmoil, because he turned to her suddenly, his eyes boring into her. He bent down and gently lifted her to her feet, his hands firm on her arms. For a long moment he stared at her, and she met his gaze, trying to fathom the emotion in his hazel eyes. "Do you trust me, Kate?" he asked softly, so softly that it might have been the wind over the water rather than his voice asking the question.

She searched his face, and it was like looking into eternity, making her pulse quicken. There was only one answer, and they both knew it. "Yes," she whispered. "God help me, I trust you with my life."

"Then believe me," he said quietly, his eyes holding hers. "Things will work out. I promise you that."

Is it in your power to promise that, she wondered with an ache in her heart. How was it possible to love him so much yet to feel such shadows between them? He pressed her against him and she felt the heat warm in her blood and loins, heat that overcame her whenever he touched her like this.

She shivered thinking of the power he had over her, but it was a power she held over him as well, she thought as she felt the heat rise in his body and the urgency of his embrace.

He loosened his hold on her, and with his arm around her shoulders guided her back to the cabin. She surrendered to the passion that always existed between them, but still there was a shadow over her, as though a ghostly presence hovered nearby.

Kate's uneasiness persisted even on the trip back, and Louise Andrews's words kept ringing in her heart. *Two different worlds, two different worlds. Leora would always be between you, like a shadow.*

Kate cast a sideways glance at Jim steering the rudder and frowned with apprehension. When he stared out over the water like that, a distant expression in his eyes, she always wondered if he was thinking about Leora. Why wouldn't he talk about her?

Kate sat in front of the TV Monday night waiting with a sense of dread for the latest news on the refinery. Buck had gone to Red's to help him repair the winch on the dredge, and Mary had dropped over to visit. Her kids were spending the night at their grandmother's, and Frank was helping

Buck and Red. Jim was supposed to come by later.

"Are you sure you don't mind having the TV on?" Kate asked, and Mary shook her head, munching on one of the sugar cookies Kate had put out with their tea.

"I'd like to see the news myself. Frank's brother is still worried about his job."

Kate nodded, only half-hearing her as the lead story came on. A picture of the refinery came up, and Mary instantly quieted as Kate turned up the sound.

"Carlisle Refineries has apparently solved its continuing problems with oil spills, and the Coast Guard and EPA have given their approval to the newly implemented improvements," the newscaster said. "Today Mark Brighton interviewed spokesman Jim Carlisle as he was leaving the refinery." A tape came up, and Kate froze when she saw the interviewer pushing a microphone at Jim — and a woman.

Jim was relaxed and smiling, telling the interviewer that new equipment had been installed, that the spills had been cleaned up, and that there were no foreseeable problems in the future. He sounded confident and tired, and he looked wonderful, but Kate registered all that dully. Her eyes were on the woman beside him, who looked so familiar, like a figure from her dreams.

Her senses focused again when the interviewer said, "Thank you, Mr. Carlisle," and she watched Jim's hand touch the woman's waist, propelling her toward the Porsche.

She had long, blonde, permed hair and a breezy smile, and she was dressed immaculately in a pale blue suit with ruffled blouse. She was stunning. Kate felt that she knew her, but not quite.

The interviewer turned toward the camera. "That was Jim Carlisle with a friend identified as Mariette Mason. From Carlisle Refineries, this is Mark Brighton."

Mariette Mason! Leora's sister! What was Jim doing with her? As soon as she asked herself the question, Kate felt her heart sink.

Louise had been right. Jim would always be tied to Leora in one way or another. It was useless to pretend otherwise.

Kate suddenly realized that Mary had put on her coat and was hurrying to the door. "I'll see you tomorrow, Kate. Thanks for the tea. I can't wait to call Frank's brother and see if he heard about the refinery. It's such good news."

"Yes, it sure is," Kate said, smiling dully as the door closed.

She didn't know how long she sat staring

into space, but she roused when she heard a knock at the door.

"What's wrong?" Jim asked immediately, frowning when he stepped inside. "You look upset."

"I'm so glad that everything worked out at the refinery," Kate said in brittle tones, turning her back on him to stare out the window at the blackness.

"You don't sound glad," Jim muttered.

"You're so good on TV, Jim. You manage to make everything sound so wonderful. Jim Carlisle solves the world's problems." She spun around, fixing him with an angry stare. "You're a real miracle worker."

"Perhaps you'd be happier if the government had closed down the refinery," he said dryly.

"Don't be absurd."

"Is that so absurd, Kate?" His lips twisted sardonically. "I think you hate the refinery so much that you're threatened by my involvement in it."

Kate stared back at him, stunned. "All right," she said in a shaking voice, "it's partly the refinery — yes! I don't know if I can live with that side of your life."

Jim pushed his hair back in exasperation. "I never expected you to live with the refinery. What I planned —"

"I don't want to hear your plans," Kate burst out, interrupting him. Her voice cracked. "I don't think I could stand it, to hear you tell me about the wonderful times we'd have at your aunt's parties and the luncheons I'd give for the wives of your business acquaintances. Maybe we could even go to the Civic Society's Christmas dance. Who knows — we might even be chosen king and queen. That is if they'd let me in in my oilskin apron with mud on my face." Her voice ended on a high squeak as tears scalded her eyes. She felt as though the world was grinding to a halt.

"I told you I don't like those kind of functions," Jim ground out. "Don't you believe anything I say, Kate? I thought you trusted me. Have you changed so much since you said that?"

"I don't know what I believe anymore," she said in a low voice. "But when I saw you with Mariette Mason I felt like I'd been kicked in the stomach."

"Mariette?" he repeated incredulously. "I saw her once today as she was leaving the plant. She came to see my uncle about some benefit. What on earth has she got to do with us?"

"Everything," Kate hissed. "She's Leora's sister, and I can't help comparing myself with her and thinking about what kind of life you're accustomed to living. Somehow I don't think it includes oyster tonging on a common skiff."

When she saw him blanch, her stomach turned to ice. He didn't live in her world, and she couldn't live in his.

"Kate."

"No!" She turned her back again so she wouldn't have to see him, but he was mirrored in the window. "Don't tell me any more pretty stories, Jim. Just leave. Please."

"All right." His voice was cold, and the reflection in the window showed his brows knit in a furious scowl. "You have some crazy idea that you and I don't belong together, and you're determined to prove it. If that's what you want, Kate, then that's what you can have. I could tell you about the refinery and about Leora, but you don't really want to hear it. If you can't believe in us, then why should I? I'm leaving now. You can sleep with your so-called trust tonight, Kate. I hope it keeps you warm."

She stood paralyzed as she heard the door slam behind him, and then the tears welled over. Her life had just shattered, flinging her out into space to drift alone and helpless.

The next morning found Kate dry-eyed

and collected as she stared out the window toward the Chesapeake. The mournful honking of a flock of Canada geese landing in the marsh floated toward her. The sound seemed especially sad this morning. Gray light filtered through the window, and even the pale pink sunrise seemed muted.

Kate had cried out all her tears the night before as she'd lain on the couch unable to sleep. She'd muffled her sobs in the pillow, but Fudge had come in and touched her shoulder with his nose, offering silent sympathy.

An anguished sleep had claimed her near dawn, but it gave scarce relief from her torment. In her dreams Louise Andrews was telling her again and again that she and Jim were from two different worlds. And when Kate reached for him, he turned and walked away.

Kate was dressed now, her jeans and faded plaid shirt providing enough warmth for the chill of the kitchen but none for the chill in her heart. She'd scrambled some eggs, but they sat untouched on her plate while she stared out the window.

She searched through the mail on the table and pulled out the letter about the job interview. Wilmington. At least it was far away from Jim.

★ ★ ★

Kate's bags were by the door when Buck got up later that morning, and he stopped short. "You and Jim elopin'?" he asked, then he saw her face and immediately sobered. "What is it, Katie?"

"I've got to leave, Buck," she said quietly.

"What's all this about?" he asked. "Where are you going?"

"I'm going to interview for the Wilmington job," she said.

He relaxed then, his features sagging into tiredness. "When should I tell Jim you'll be back?"

"I won't be back, Buck," she said, watching surprise register on his face. "If I don't get that job, then I'm going to stay there and get another. Please don't tell Jim where I've gone."

Buck's jaw sagged, and it was a minute before he spoke. "It's not like you to run out, Katie," he said. "Whatever happened between you and Jim, can't you face it and work it out?"

She shook her head vehemently. "It's just not something that can be worked out. You and I both know I can't stay here forever and tong oysters. It's time I moved on anyway."

Buck shook his head. "You know you

263

won't be happy away from the Chesapeake," he warned.

"Then I'll just have to learn to be unhappy like most of the rest of the world," she said crisply. "Listen, I've got to get going now so I can get in before dark. You take care, and I'll phone to let you know where I'm staying."

He nodded, his eyes looking tired and old, and Kate suddenly hated to go. But this was the way it had always been with her and Buck. They were both fiercely independent, and they came and went as they chose. She gave him a quick kiss on his leathery cheek and went out the door.

chapter

12

A blast from a nearby stereo woke Kate, but it was a moment before she remembered that she wasn't home. She was in the Wilmington apartment she'd rented two days ago, and she'd apparently survived another near-sleepless night.

Maybe she should make a slash mark on the wall for each night she spent here. That's what all the jail inmates did in those late-night movies. And she certainly felt as if she was in jail. Actually it was worse than jail because she was forced to endure the stereo next door.

She'd called Buck the night before to let him know where she was, and eventually he'd brought up the topic of Jim. "He came by last night, Katie, and when I told him you was gone, he looked furious enough to put his fist through the door. Then he just turned around and left. Ain't seen him since."

Kate had swallowed, her throat constricted painfully. "Thanks, Buck."

"You okay, Katie?"

"Sure. I'm always okay."

"That's just it," Buck said. "You take it on the chin like some prizefighter, and then you walk around like you ain't hurt at all. You've done that all your life, honey. Don't you think it's about time you stopped pretendin' you're fine when you ain't?"

"I'm just tired." Kate sighed wearily. "But thanks for worrying about me."

But she knew Buck was right. She hurt badly. The problem was that no one could help.

Another blast of the stereo brought Kate back to the present. At least the constant roar of rock music from the next apartment kept her mind off her aching heart.

She thought for a moment that she was hearing a keyboard solo coming over the stereo, then she realized it was the ringing of her phone. It might be the elderly woman downstairs. She'd knocked on the door three times in the last two days, asking Kate to turn down the stereo. After several vain attempts to explain that the noise wasn't coming from her apartment, Kate had given up and apologized for the disturbance.

"Hello?" She sighed in resignation.

"Is this Kate Flannery?"

It took Kate a moment to recognize Louise Andrews's voice. Then she sank down on the couch. "How did you get my number?"

"From your grandfather. I'm sorry to bother you, but I had to talk to you."

"Is something wrong?" Kate's throat constricted, her heart pounding. "Is Jim all right?"

"To tell you the truth, I'm worried about him. He quit his job."

"Quit his job?" Kate repeated dazedly. It was the last thing she expected to hear. "But why?"

"I don't know. I thought you might have some idea."

"No, we haven't talked." Kate hesitated, then added, "We've gone our separate ways."

There was a long silence on the other end, and Kate's pulse kept time with the steady *thump, thump* of the music next door. "I thought maybe you could talk to him," Louise said, a thread of desperation in her voice. "He'd listen to you. I'm sure of it."

"I'm sorry. I don't think I could do that."

She could sense the last of Louise's hope ebbing away in her sigh. "Somehow I felt that if anyone could reach him, it would be you." There was a long pause. "I suppose not. Well, good-bye."

Kate replaced the receiver and leaned back against the couch.

Jim . . .

He'd quit his job — why? Just the thought of him made her blood run hot, and her pulse rapidly outpaced the stereo beat. She wouldn't think about him. She wouldn't!

But she'd thought of nothing *but* Jim since she'd left Tilghman Island. Every time she looked out her window at the small patch of sky that was visible, she thought of the sky over the Chesapeake. And that brought a whole flood of memories — Jim's voice saying her name, his hands driving her senses to sweet oblivion, his lips coaxing hers to passionate response. No wonder she couldn't sleep — she was here and he was there, and she was absolutely miserable.

She'd pulled herself together after her divorce, and she'd forged a strong, independent life for herself. She'd willed away her disappointment and pain. But it seemed that this time she'd run into something stronger than her will — her need for Jim.

She'd fought long and hard to hide her vulnerability, and now it was keeping her from what she wanted. She was afraid to risk being hurt again. Damn! It wasn't possible to hurt any more than she did now.

The logical side of her brain ticked off the reasons it wouldn't work — the same reasons she'd recited each night before going to sleep. But her heart refused to listen. So what if she wasn't born to the silver spoon? For Jim, she would damn well learn to wear silk and like goose liver and to make small talk over vodka martinis. All that mattered was that she did those things with him.

An hour later she was driving home to Tilghman Island. A light snow began to fall, and by the time she turned into her driveway, the ground was hidden under a powdery coating.

Fudge came barreling out the door behind Buck, nearly knocking him down in his haste to reach Kate first. She bent to scratch the dog behind his ears, laughing at his enthusiasm, then stood up and smiled at Buck.

"Did you come to visit?" he asked, his eyes crinkling in pleasure.

"No." She laughed. "I came to my senses."

As soon as she'd dumped her suitcase in the bedroom, she called Jim's apartment, but there was no answer. She tried every fifteen minutes for an hour, growing more fidgety with each call. She paced the kitchen, staring out the window. The snow had stopped falling, but the sky was gray and hung low with clouds. The bare branches of the trees were starkly silhouetted. "I think I might take the skiff out," she said on an impulse, turning to Buck.

He looked up from his magazine, his eyebrows raised. "Alone?"

She nodded. "I need to get out on the water by myself. Okay?"

He nodded. "Yeah. I know how it is. Go on."

"Thanks. See you later." She hurried to get her red windbreaker with the warm lining and her red knit cap, then raced out the door. Her nervousness grew on the drive to the dock, and she fairly ran to the skiff.

The wind was picking up when she edged the *Kathryn D* out onto the Chesapeake. Kate felt her heartbeat matching the throbbing of the engine. She set her course without thought and let the skiff carry her away from all her troubles. Out here on the Chesapeake she suddenly felt free again, and the pain she'd kept bottled up inside began to surface. The wind stung her face as the tears flowed, but she let them come, feeling release. She stopped the boat and rubbed her wet eyes with her coat sleeve, the wind swirling around her. She looked around and got her bearings, each marsh and shoreline learned from years of experience. The irony of it hit her then — she was almost precisely at the spot where the engine had died that time and she'd fallen overboard.

The sound of honking geese reached her, and she looked up to see the familiar V formation overhead. Suddenly the isolation and beauty overwhelmed her and she began to cry again. This time, before she could stop herself, his name welled up from deep inside her. "Jim," she sobbed, turning her face to the sky. "Jim." The only answer was the wind and the first few tentative snowflakes from an approaching storm.

Then from farther up the bay came the sound of a boat motor, muted in the wind. It was coming toward her. She hastily wiped her eyes again, but the tears were still streaming down her face. She stood stoically waiting for the boat to pass, her back to it, but the motor slowed, and she cursed under her breath, waiting for someone to holler and ask if she was okay.

Then the motor was cut, and Kate turned around to tell the intruder that she was fine, and she was about to start back. But she froze where she stood. Standing in the small motorboat that was now drifting within three feet of the skiff was Jim. She stared at him, feeling as though she were looking at an apparition as the snow picked up and blew his unruly brown curls. He wore the same black windbreaker and jeans, and his face looked hard, angry, and dangerous. He apparently hadn't shaved in the days since she'd seen him, and there were dark circles under his eyes as though he hadn't slept.

Suddenly she was afraid of him and of the strong emotions just the sight of him had awakened in her. "Stay away from my boat," she ordered shakily as the motorboat bumped the skiff.

"I'm boarding the *Kathryn D* whether you like it or not," came back his sharp reply. "So stand aside."

There was nothing she could do as he tied the boat fast against the skiff and leaped lithely aboard. He stood staring at her, hands on hips, his features forbidding. "I've chased you halfway down the bay, Kate Flannery," he said in a low voice. "When I went to your house and Buck told me you were out here, I thought I'd go crazy if I didn't catch you. And now that I have, we're going to talk."

He took a step toward her, and she backed up instinctively. There was a dangerous air about him, as though he were holding himself in check. She took another step back, and her foot caught on a rope. She stumbled, and in that short instant he was beside her, his hand closing around her arm. The next moment he was pulling her into the cabin and slamming the door shut.

"You look like you haven't slept worth a damn," he muttered, paying no attention to her futile struggles to free her arm.

Tired of the battle, Kate stood stiffly and glared at him. "You have no right coming on board my boat like a pirate, acting like I've committed some crime."

"Does my presence bother you that much?" he drawled in a taunting voice, one finger tracing a line down her cheek. She swallowed convulsively and his lips twisted in a crooked smile with no humor. "Because being this close to you sure as hell bothers me," he said softly.

Kate felt her breath catch in her throat, and suddenly the tension left her body. "These last few days have been murder," she whispered. His arms went around her, and Kate melted against his chest.

"We have to talk," he murmured, his jaw moving against her head.

"I just want to be with you." Her hands slipped inside his windbreaker to stroke his chest, and she reveled in the suddenly uneven cadence of his breathing. "I don't care about the refinery or your aunt or anything else. That's why I came back. I just want you."

She felt his ragged sigh against her hair, then he was tilting her face up to his, his lips moving hungrily over her cheeks and mouth. "Kate," he groaned, burying his mouth against her throat, his hand curving over her breast, "I don't want any doubts about us."

"I don't have any," she said as his heated caress transmitted sensual pleasure to every inch of her flesh.

"But I want you to know the truth about everything," he said. "Come here." He pulled her gently to the table and sat down beside her, holding her hands in his. His thumb stroked her palm as he spoke, and Kate realized that whatever he said, she would love him no less. He'd taught her to trust again, and she knew that what she and Jim shared could endure.

"Kate," he began, "I've never told another soul about this. It's something I've carried with me this last year, something that's eaten me up inside, so much so that I couldn't even talk to you about it. But you've become such a part of me, so much of my life and so much that's good and right, that I want to tell you everything about it."

"Leora?" she asked softly.

He nodded. "I was in love with her at first," he said quietly. "She was pretty and full of life. But after we were married I found out that was all on the surface. Leora had been catered to by her family and she wanted her own way all the time. When she didn't get it, she was mean and vindictive. She insisted we live in California, so I stayed there for her. But that wasn't enough. She wanted more money, more excitement, more glamour." He paused and took a deep breath. "Our fights got worse and worse. Each time she'd storm out of the house in a rage instead of trying to resolve anything. I'd finally had enough, and I told her I wanted a divorce. She ran out of the house, and I went after her. I jumped into the passenger side of the car just as she took off."

Kate waited, knowing what he was going to say, but knowing he had to say it, to finally voice it out loud. "She was driving like a maniac, and I couldn't calm her down. The car left the road and hit a tree. I was only slightly injured. She was killed instantly."

Jim's grip on Kate's hands eased as though the worst was over for him. "I never told her family or mine the truth about our marriage or that accident. It was kinder to let them think we'd been happy. So I became quite a cynic — until I met a gorgeous oyster tonger who turned my life upside down." He smiled and stroked her hair back from her face. "You really are something, you know that?"

"Me?" She laughed shakily. "You've kept me off balance from the day you first stepped onto this boat."

Then another thought struck her, and she sobered. "Will you go back to your job now?"

"The refinery?" he said in surprise. "How did you find out about that?" He closed his eyes wearily. "My aunt, of course." He looked at her searchingly. "No, I've accomplished what I wanted to there. I've updated the equipment and set things up so there won't be any more pollution problems. No, I've had something else in the back of my mind for some time now." He grinned down at her. "How would you like to go into business with me?"

"What?"

"I'm starting my own consulting firm for pollution control, and there's an opening for a bright young lady with a degree in marine biology who would do research on the Chesapeake. Of course, that's providing the young lady in question won't make me call her captain." She laughed, and Jim said solemnly, "One more condition. I want you to marry me, Kate. I think you know how much I love you. If you say no, I'll commit a real act of piracy and force-feed you croquettes until you say yes."

Her laughter was free and happy when she said yes, yes again and again against his mouth and neck and jaw as he held her to him, raining kisses on her face.

"I guess this means I'll have to develop a taste for junk food," he said wryly.

"Don't worry," she promised him mockingly. "We've always got Jeeves."

"I think we can do without Jeeves quite nicely."

"Yes, quite nicely." Her words were almost lost in his kiss, and she felt suddenly alive and starved for his love.

"You know," he whispered against her ear, "there's quite a snow storm on the way. In fact, we may have to spend tonight in a certain cove near here."

"Too bad," she murmured without a trace of regret. The skiff was rocking in the wind, and lacy snowflakes drifted past the cabin window.

"We won't be rich," he added quietly. "At least not at first."

"Just when I was beginning to grow accustomed to the lap of luxury," Kate whispered teasingly.

Jim began to unbutton her coat slowly, his eyes traveling over her face as though memorizing something precious. A piece of crumpled paper fell from her pocket, and Kate recognized the limerick she'd written for him, then forgotten. Jim picked it up and looked at it, then a slow grin spread over his face, and he read aloud.

> *"There once was a man named Jim*
> *Who tonged with great vigor and vim.*
> *His prowess in bed*
> *Was so phenomenal, it's said*
> *That the oysters took lessons from him."*

He threw his head back, and his laughter echoed out over the Chesapeake, the only sound in a dusky evening filling slowly with snowflakes. "Come here," he said huskily. "Let's teach the oysters a thing or two."

We hope you have enjoyed this Large Print book. Other Thorndike Press or Chivers Press Large Print books are available at your library or directly from the publishers.

For more information about current and upcoming titles, please call or write, without obligation, to:

Thorndike Press
295 Kennedy Memorial Drive
Waterville, ME 04901 USA
Tel. (800) 223-1244

OR

Chivers Press Limited
Windsor Bridge Road
Bath BA2 3AX
England
Tel. (0225) 335336

All our Large Print titles are designed for easy reading, and all our books are made to last.